Hector and the
Search for Happiness

François Lelord

François Lelord has had a successful career as a psychiatrist both in the United States and France. He now devotes his time to writing, and is the author (in conjunction with Christophe André) of a number of best-selling self-help books.

Lorenza Garcia

Lorenza Garcia translates from French and Spanish. Her most recent translation is *The Divine Blood* by Andrea H. Japp. She currently lives in London.

Hector and the
Search for Happiness

Hector and the Search for Happiness

François Lelord

Translated by Lorenza Garcia

Gallic Books
London

This book is supported by the French ministry of foreign Affairs as part of the Burgess Programme run by the Cultural Department of the French Embassy in London.

www.frenchbooknews.com

Liberté • Égalité • Fraternité
RÉPUBLIQUE FRANÇAISE

A Gallic Book

First published in France as *Le Voyage d'Hector ou la recherche du bonheur* by Odile Jacob

First published in Great Britain in 2010 by Gallic Books,
134 Lots Road, London, SW10 0RJ

A CIP record for this book is available from the British Library

ISBN 978-1-906040-23-9

Typeset in Fournier MT by SX Composing DTP, Rayleigh, Essex
Printed and bound by CPI Bookmarque, Croydon, CR0 4TD

2 4 6 8 10 9 7 5 3

HECTOR IS DISSATISFIED

ONCE upon a time there was a young psychiatrist called Hector who was not very satisfied with himself.

Hector was not very satisfied with himself, even though he looked just like a real psychiatrist: he wore little round glasses that made him look intellectual; he knew how to listen to people sympathetically, saying 'mmm'; he even had a little moustache, which he twirled when he was thinking very hard.

His consulting room also looked just like a real psychiatrist's. There was an old couch (a present from his mother when he moved in), copies of Egyptian and Hindu statuettes, and a large bookcase full of complicated books, some of them so complicated he had not even read them.

Many people wanted to make an appointment with Hector, not just because he looked like a real psychiatrist, but because he had a gift that all good doctors have and that you can't simply learn at college: he really was interested in people.

The first time people go to a psychiatrist, they're often a bit embarrassed. They worry the psychiatrist will think they're mad even though they know he's used to it. Or else they worry that he won't think their case is serious enough and will tell them to take their troubles elsewhere. But since they've made the appointment and kept it, they decide to recount their odd little quirks, the strange thoughts they haven't told anyone about before but that make them unhappy, the great fears or deep sorrows that prevent them from living life to the full. They also worry that they won't express themselves properly and that they will be boring. And it must be said that sometimes psychiatrists do look bored, or tired. If you weren't used to it you might wonder if they really were listening to you.

But with Hector it was almost never like that. He looked at people as they told their story, he nodded in encouragement, made his little 'mmm-hmm' noises, twirled his moustache and sometimes he'd even say, 'Wait, explain that again. I didn't quite understand.' Except on days when he was very tired, people really felt that Hector was listening to what they had to say and finding it interesting.

So people came back to see him, they made lots of appointments, gave his name to their friends, and mentioned him to their doctors, who sent other patients to him. And soon Hector spent long days listening to people and had a lot of tax to pay, even though he didn't charge much for a consultation. (His mother was always telling him he should charge more, but he didn't feel he should.)

He charged less for his consultations, for example, than Madame Irina, who was quite a well-known psychic. She would say to him, 'Doctor, you should put up your fees.'

'So I've been told,' Hector would reply.

'I'm saying it for your own good, Doctor, I can see what's best for you.'

'I'm sure you can. And how are you seeing these days?'

It should be explained that Madame Irina had come to consult Hector because she could no longer see into the future.

Her heart had been broken when a man had left her, and ever since then she couldn't see properly any more. As she was clever, she was able to find interesting things to tell her clients. But as she was not completely dishonest either, it troubled her not being able to see as before. And so Hector had given her pills for people who feel very sad, and gradually she was regaining her ability to see.

Hector didn't know what to make of it.

He wasn't just successful because he knew how to listen to people. He also knew all the tricks of his trade.

First of all, he knew how to answer a question with another question. For example, when people asked him, 'Do you think I'm going to get better, Doctor?' he would reply: 'What does "getting better" mean to you?' In this way Hector helped people to think about their own case and find their own ways of getting better.

He also knew all about medication. In psychiatry that's quite simple since there are only four main types of medication that can be prescribed: pills to take when you're sad – anti-depressants; pills to take when you're scared – tranquillisers; pills to take when you have very strange thoughts and hear voices – anti-psychotics; and then pills to avoid highs that are too high or lows that are too low – mood stabilisers. Actually, it's a bit more complicated than that because for each type of medication there are at least ten different brands of pill, all with funny-sounding names that have been made up specially, and the psychiatrist's job is to find the most suitable one for his patient. Pills are a bit like sweets: not everybody likes the same ones.

And when medication wasn't enough, or when people had no need for it, Hector had another way of helping them: psychotherapy. A complicated name for simply helping people by listening and talking to them. Not just talking to them any old how, but following a special method. As with pills, there are different types of psychotherapy, some of them invented by people who have been dead a long time. Hector had learnt a method of psychotherapy invented by people who were still alive, if rather old. According to this method, the psychiatrist talked to the patients as well as listening to them and this went down well, especially with those who had encountered psychiatrists who barely spoke to them, which they simply couldn't get used to.

In Madame Irina's case, Hector hadn't used much psychotherapy because whenever he was about to ask her a question she would say, 'I know what you're going to ask me, Doctor.'

The worst of it was that she was often (but not always) right.

And so, using the tricks of his trade – medication, psycho-therapy and his gift of being genuinely interested in people – Hector was quite a good psychiatrist. That's to say, he was as successful as any good doctor, a cardiologist for example. He managed to cure some of his patients completely. Others he kept in good health provided they took their medication every day and came to talk to him from time to time. And finally there were some patients whom he merely managed to help live with their condition by making it as bearable as possible.

*

And yet Hector felt dissatisfied.

He felt dissatisfied because he could see perfectly well that he couldn't make people happy.

HECTOR HAS DOUBTS

Hector's practice was in a city full of wide avenues lined with attractive old buildings. This city differed from most of the world's big cities: the inhabitants had plenty to eat; if they were ill they could receive free medical treatment; children went to school, and most people had a job. They could also go to lots of different showings at the cinema that weren't too expensive; there were museums, swimming pools and even special places to ride bicycles without being run over. People could also watch lots of different TV channels, read all sorts of newspapers, and journalists were free to write almost whatever they wanted. People had plenty of time off, even though this could be a problem for those who didn't have enough money to go away on holiday.

Because, although everything worked better than in most of the world's big cities, there were still some people who had only just enough money to live on, and some children who couldn't stand school and behaved very badly, or didn't even have parents to look after them any more. There were also grown-ups who were out of work and who were so unhappy that they tried to make themselves feel better by drinking anything and everything or by taking very bad pills. But those people didn't live in the type of neighbourhood where Hector worked. Hector knew they existed because he had treated a lot of them when he worked at the hospital. And since then, he'd continued going to the hospital every Wednesday instead of going to his practice. And that's where he saw people like Roger, for example, whom he asked, 'Have you been taking your medication, Roger?'

'Yes, yes, the Lord is my shepherd, He leadeth me.'

'I'm sure he does, but have you been taking your medication?'

'Yes, yes, the Lord is my shepherd, He leadeth me.'

You see, Roger believed that the Good Lord talked to him constantly, what they call hearing voices, and he would reply out loud. What's wrong with that? you may ask. The problem was that when Roger didn't take his medication, he would talk to himself in the street – sometimes in a very loud voice if he'd had a drink – and unkind people would laugh at him. As he was quite a big fellow this occasionally ended in trouble, and Roger would find himself back in the psychiatric hospital for a long time.

Roger had a lot of other problems: he'd never had a mother and father to look after him, he hadn't done well at school, and since he'd begun talking to the Good Lord nobody wanted to employ him. And so Hector, together with a lady from social services, had filled in loads of forms so that Roger could stay in his tiny studio flat in a neighbourhood you wouldn't necessarily have wanted to live in.

At Hector's practice it was very different from the hospital: the people who came to see him there had done quite well at school, had been brought up by a mother and a father, and had a job. Or if they lost their job they quite easily found another.

They generally dressed nicely and knew how to tell their story without making grammatical errors and the women were often quite pretty (which was sometimes a problem for Hector).

Some of them had real disorders or had suffered real misfortune, and in this case Hector generally succeeded in treating them using psychotherapy and medication. But a lot of them had no real disorders – or at least none that Hector had learnt to treat when he was a student – and hadn't suffered any real misfortune either – like having unkind parents or losing somebody really close to them. And yet, these people weren't happy.

Take Adeline, for example, quite an attractive young woman whom Hector saw quite often.

'How are you?' Hector would ask.

'Are you hoping that one day I'll say: "Very well"?'

'Why do you think I'd hope that?'

'You must be getting rather fed up with my problems.'

She wasn't far wrong, even though Hector was actually quite fond of Adeline. She was successful in her work which was to sell things – that's to say, she knew how to sell things for a lot more than they were worth, and consequently her bosses were delighted and often gave her large bonuses.

And yet she never stopped complaining, especially about men. As she was really rather charming, she always had a man in her life, but it never worked out: either they were nice but she didn't find them very exciting; or they were exciting but she didn't find them particularly nice, or they were neither nice nor exciting and she wondered why she was with them at all. She had found a way of making the exciting men nicer and that was by leaving them. But then, of course, they weren't exciting any more either. In addition, all these men were successful, because if a man wasn't successful he didn't stand a chance with Adeline.

Just by asking Adeline questions, Hector tried to make her understand that the height of happiness did not necessarily come from having the most excitement with a very successful man who is also very nice (especially as you can imagine how easy it is to find a very successful man who is also very nice!) But it was difficult, Adeline had very high standards.

Hector had quite a few patients like Adeline.

He also saw men who thought like Adeline: they wanted the most exciting woman who was also successful and nice. And at work it was the same: they wanted a very important job, but one that would allow them the freedom to 'fulfil themselves' – as some of them put it. Even when they were successful in their jobs they still wondered whether they wouldn't have been much happier doing something else.

Basically, all of these well-dressed people said that they didn't like their lives, they questioned their choice of profession, they wondered whether they were married or nearly married to the right person, they had the impression that they were missing out on something important in life, that time was passing and they couldn't be everything that they wanted to be.

They weren't happy, and it was no joke because some of them had thoughts of suicide, and Hector had to pay special attention to them.

He began wondering whether he didn't attract that particular type of person. Perhaps there was something about his way of talking which they especially liked? Or about the way he twirled his moustache as he looked at them, or even about his Hindu statuettes? Which was why they passed on his address, and more and more of them turned up at his practice. He casually asked his more experienced colleagues if they only treated people with real disorders. Hector's colleagues looked at him as if he'd asked rather a silly question. Of course they didn't only treat people with real disorders! They also saw a lot of people who were dissatisfied with their lives and who felt unhappy. And from what they told him, Hector understood that they didn't have much more success than him.

What was even stranger was that in those neighbourhoods where most people were much more fortunate than people living elsewhere, there were more psychiatrists than in all the other neighbourhoods put together, and every month new ones arrived! In fact, if you looked at a world map of psychiatrists (they're very hard to find so don't even try), you'd see that in countries like the one where Hector lived, there were far more psychiatrists than in the rest of the world, where there were nevertheless far more people.

That was all very interesting, but it was of no use to Hector. He felt that he wasn't helping these unhappy people. Even though they liked coming back to see him, he was finding it more and more of a strain. He had noticed that he was far more tired after seeing people who were dissatisfied with their lives than after seeing patients like Roger. And since he was seeing more and more people who were unhappy for no apparent reason, he was becoming more and more tired, and even a little unhappy himself. He began to wonder whether he was in the right profession, whether he was happy with his life, whether he wasn't missing out on something. And then he felt very afraid because he wondered whether these unhappy people were contagious. He even thought about taking pills himself (he knew some of his colleagues took them), but on reflection he decided that it wasn't a good solution.

One day Madame Irina said to him, 'Doctor, I can see that you're very tired.'

'Oh, I'm sorry if it shows.'

'You should take a holiday, it would do you good.'

Hector thought that this was a good idea: why didn't he go on holiday?

But being a conscientious young man, he would plan his holiday so that it would help him to become a better psychiatrist. He would take what they call a busman's holiday.

And so he decided to take a trip around the world, and everywhere he went he would try to understand what made people happy or unhappy. That way, he told himself, if there was a secret of happiness, he'd be sure to find it.

HECTOR MAKES AN IMPORTANT DISCOVERY

HECTOR announced to his patients that he was going away on holiday.

When they heard the news, some of them, often those with the most serious disorders, said to him, 'You're absolutely right, Doctor, with the job you do you need a rest!' But others seemed slightly put out that Hector was going on holiday. They said to him, 'So, I won't be able to see you for several weeks?' They were generally the unhappy people whom Hector couldn't make happy and who were wearing him out.

Hector had a good friend, Clara, and he also had to tell her that he was going away on holiday. He asked her whether she would like to go with him, not just to be polite, but because he liked Clara a lot and they both felt they didn't spend enough time together.

Hector and Clara loved each other, but they found it difficult to make plans together. For example, sometimes it was Clara who wanted to get married and have a baby and sometimes it was Hector, but they almost never wanted it at the same time.

Clara worked very hard for a big company – a pharmaceutical company that produced the pills psychiatrists prescribe. In fact, that's how she'd met Hector, at a conference organised to present the latest products to psychiatrists, and in particular the wonderful new pill her company had just invented.

Clara was paid a lot of money to come up with names for pills that would appeal to psychiatrists and their patients all over the world. And also to make them believe that the pills her company made were better than those made by other companies.

Although she was still very young she was already successful and the proof of this was that when Hector rang her at the office, he was almost never able to speak to her because she was always in a meeting. And when she and Hector went away for the weekend, she would take work to finish on her laptop while he went out for walks on his own or fell asleep beside her on the bed.

When Hector suggested to Clara that she go with him, she said that she couldn't just leave like that out of the blue, because she had to go to meetings to decide on the name for the new pill her company was making (which would be better than all the other pills that had ever been made since the beginning of time).

Hector didn't say anything; he understood. But he was still slightly put out. He wondered whether going away together wasn't actually more important than meetings to find a name for a new pill. But since his profession was to understand other people's points of view, he simply said to Clara: 'That's all right, I understand.'

Later, while they were having dinner at a restaurant, Clara told Hector how complicated life was at her office. She had two bosses who both liked her, but who didn't like each other. This made it very difficult for Clara, because when she worked for one boss there was always a risk she might upset the other boss, and vice versa when she worked for the first boss, if you follow.

Hector didn't really see why she had two bosses at the same time, but Clara explained that it was because of something called 'matrix management'. Hector thought that this sounded like an expression invented by psychiatrists, and so he wasn't surprised that it created complicated situations and drove people a bit crazy.

He still hadn't told Clara the real reason for his holiday, because since the beginning of their dinner it had mostly been Clara talking about her problems at work.

But as he was growing a little tired of this, he decided to begin his investigation into what made people happy or unhappy straight away. When Clara stopped talking in order to finish her meal, Hector looked at her and said, 'Are you happy?'

Clara put down her fork and looked at Hector. She seemed upset. She said, 'Do you want to leave me?'

And Hector saw that her eyes were shining – like when people are about to cry. He put his hand on hers and said: no, of course not (although actually there had been times when he had thought about it), he had only asked her that because he was beginning his investigation.

Clara seemed reassured, though not completely, and Hector explained why he wanted to understand better what made people a little happy or unhappy. But now there was another thing he wanted to understand, and that was why when he'd asked Clara whether she was happy she'd thought that Hector wanted to leave her.

She told him that she'd taken it as a criticism. As if Hector had said: 'You'll never be happy' and that therefore he wouldn't want to stay with her, because, obviously, nobody wants to live with a person who'll never be happy. Hector assured her that this was not at all what he'd meant. In order to put Clara's mind completely at rest, he joked around and made her laugh, and this time they both felt in love at the same time until the end of the meal and even afterwards when they went home to bed.

Later, as he was falling asleep beside her, he told himself that his investigation had got off to a good start, that he'd already discovered two things.

One of them he already knew, but it was good to be reminded of it: women are very complicated, even if you are a psychiatrist.

The other would be very useful to him during his investigation: you must be careful when you ask people whether they're happy; it's a question that can upset them a great deal.

HECTOR GOES TO CHINA

HECTOR decided to go to China. He'd never been there before, and it seemed to him like a good place to think about happiness. He remembered the adventures of Tintin in *The Blue Lotus*, and Tintin's friend Chang's adoptive father, Mr Wang. The wise old Chinaman with his long white beard looked as if he might have a few interesting things to say about happiness, and there had to be people like him still in China today. Also, in *The Blue Lotus* this distinguished gentleman's son goes crazy and makes his parents very unhappy. When they cry Tintin tries to comfort them, but he doesn't really succeed. Fortunately, later on he manages to free from the clutches of villains a famous Chinese professor, who manages to cure Mr Wang's son. In the end everybody is happy, and perhaps it was reading this moving adventure as a boy that first gave Hector the idea of becoming a psychiatrist (even though he'd never heard of the word then). Hector had also seen quite a few Chinese films at the cinema with Clara, and he'd noticed that Chinese women were very pretty, even though there weren't that many in *The Blue Lotus*.

When he boarded the aeroplane, the air hostess gave him some good news: the airline had overbooked the part of the plane where Hector was supposed to be sitting, and she was giving him a seat in the part where you normally had to pay a lot more. That part of the plane is called business class, just to make it seem as if the people sitting there are travelling on business and not for the pleasure of having a nice comfortable seat, champagne and their own private TV screen.

Hector felt very happy to be there. His seat really was very comfortable, the air hostesses had brought him champagne, and he also felt they were smiling at him a lot – much more than when he travelled the normal way – but that might have been the effect of the champagne.

As the plane climbed higher and higher in the sky, he began thinking about happiness. Why did he feel so happy to be there?

Of course, he was able to stretch out comfortably, drink champagne and relax. But he could do the same thing at home in his favourite armchair, and although it was enjoyable it didn't make him as happy as here on this aeroplane.

He looked around. Two or three other people were smiling and looking around, and he thought that like him they must have had a nice surprise. He turned to the man next to him. He was reading a newspaper in English containing rows of numbers, with a serious expression on his face. He hadn't taken the champagne that the air hostess had offered him. He was a bit older than Hector, a bit fatter, too, and he wore a tie with little pictures of kangaroos on it, and so Hector thought that he wasn't going on holiday, but was travelling on business.

Later on, they started talking. The man's name was Charles, and he asked Hector if this was his first trip to China. Hector said it was. Charles told him that he knew China a little because he owned factories there, where Chinese people worked for less money than in the country Hector and Charles came from. 'For less money but just as hard!' he added.

In these factories, they made all sorts of things for children: furniture, toys and electronic games. Charles was married and had three children; they always had plenty of toys because their father owned factories that made them!

Hector had never really understood much about economics, but he asked Charles whether it wasn't inconvenient to have all those things made by the Chinese and whether it might not take jobs away from the people in Hector and Charles's country.

A few, perhaps, Charles explained, but if he employed workers in his country, his toys would be so much more expensive than those made in other countries that nobody would buy them anyway, so it would be pointless even to try. 'That's globalisation for you,' Charles concluded. Hector reflected that this was the first time during his journey that he'd heard the word globalisation, but it would surely not be the last. Charles added that one good thing was that the Chinese were becoming less poor and soon they would be able to afford toys for their own children.

Hector told himself that he'd done well to choose psychiatry, since people weren't about to go off to China to discuss their problems with Chinese psychiatrists, even though they were no doubt excellent.

He asked Charles about China, in particular whether the Chinese were very different from them. Charles thought about it, and said that essentially they weren't in fact. The greatest differences were between people in the big cities and those in the countryside, but that was true in all countries. However, he did tell Hector that he was unlikely to find anybody like Chang's father there, because China had changed a lot since the days of *The Blue Lotus*.

From the very beginning of their conversation, Hector had wanted to ask Charles if he was happy, but he remembered Clara's reaction and this time he wanted to be careful. Eventually he said: 'These seats are so comfortable!' hoping that Charles might say how glad he was to be flying business class, and then they could go on to talk about happiness.

But Charles grumbled, 'Hmm, they don't extend nearly as much as the ones in first class.' And Hector understood that Charles usually flew business class, but that one day he'd been upgraded to first class (an even more expensive part of the plane) and that he'd never forgotten it.

This made Hector think. Charles and he were sitting in identical seats, and had been offered the same champagne, but Hector was much happier because he wasn't used to it. There was another difference: Charles had been expecting to fly business class, whereas for Hector it had been a pleasant surprise.

It was the first small pleasure of his trip so far, but looking at Charles, Hector began worrying. What if the next time he flew economy class he regretted not being in business class, like Charles now regretted not being in first class?

Hector told himself that he'd just learnt his first lesson. He took out the little notebook he'd bought especially and wrote:

Lesson no. 1: Making comparisons can spoil your happiness.

He thought that this wasn't a very positive first lesson, so he tried to find another. He drank some more champagne and wrote:

Lesson no. 2: Happiness often comes when least expected.

HECTOR ENJOYS A GOOD DINNER

HECTOR was very surprised when he arrived in China. Of course he hadn't expected it to look exactly like in *The Blue Lotus* (Hector is intelligent; don't forget he's a psychiatrist), but even so.

He found himself in a city full of huge modern glass towers, like the ones containing offices that had been built around his city; only this Chinese city was at the foot of a small mountain by the sea. The houses and streets were exactly the same as in Hector's country. The only difference was that instead of the people he was used to seeing, there were lots of Chinese men in grey suits walking very quickly and speaking rather loudly into their mobile phones. He saw quite a few Chinese women, too, including some very pretty ones, though not as many as in the films. They all seemed to be in a hurry, were dressed a bit like Clara, and gave the impression that when they were at the office they also had lots of meetings.

In the taxi on his way to the hotel, Hector saw only one house that looked like a proper Chinese house, with a funny-shaped roof: it was an antiques shop wedged between two huge buildings. His hotel was a glass tower that looked exactly the same as the hotels he stayed in when he was invited to conferences organised by pharmaceutical companies. He told himself that this was beginning not to feel like a holiday any more.

Fortunately, Hector had a friend called Édouard who lived in the city. They had been at secondary school together, but afterwards, instead of studying psychiatry, Édouard had become a banker, and now he had lots of silk ties with pictures of little animals on them, played golf and every day read newspapers in English full of rows of numbers, rather like Charles, except that Édouard had never been inside a factory.

Hector and Édouard met for dinner at a very fine restaurant at the top of a tower. It was wonderful; they could see the city lights and the boats on the water. But Édouard didn't seem to be paying much attention to the view – he was more interested in the wine list.

'French, Italian or Californian?' he asked Hector straight away.

Hector replied, 'What do you prefer?' Because, as previously mentioned, he knew how to answer a question with another question, and as a result Édouard knew exactly which wine to order without his help.

Édouard seemed to have aged quite a lot since Hector had last seen him. He had bags under his eyes, and jowls, and he looked very tired indeed. He explained to Hector that he worked eighty hours a week. Hector figured out that this was nearly twice the hours he worked, and he felt really sorry for Édouard: it was terrible to work so much. But when Édouard told him how much he earned, Hector figured out that it was seven times what he earned, and he didn't feel so sorry for him any more. And when he saw how much the wine Édouard had ordered cost, he told himself that it was just as well Édouard earned so much money, because otherwise how would he have been able to pay for it?

Seeing as Édouard was an old friend, Hector felt at ease about asking him if he was happy. Édouard laughed, but not the way people laugh people when they're really amused. He explained to Hector that when you worked as hard as he did, you didn't even have time to ask yourself that question. And that was exactly why he was going to resign.

'Right now?' Hector asked. He was taken aback and wondered whether Édouard had decided this suddenly after seeing how much less tired he looked than Édouard.

'No. I'll stop when I've earned six million dollars.'

Édouard explained that it was common in his job. People worked very hard and then when they'd earned enough money they resigned and did something else or did nothing at all.

'And then they're happy?' asked Hector.

Édouard thought very hard and said that the problem was that having worked that way for so many years a lot of people weren't in a very good state when they stopped: they had health problems and some of them had got into the habit of taking harmful pills in order to be able to work longer hours, and they found it difficult to do without them. Many had got divorced because of all the meetings that prevented them from seeing their wives. They worried about money (because even when you've earned a lot of money you can still lose it, especially if you order wines like Édouard every day) and often they didn't really know what to do with themselves because they'd never done anything else except work.

'But some people cope very well,' Édouard said.

'Which ones?' Hector asked.

'The ones who continue,' Édouard replied.

And he stopped talking in order to study the label on the bottle of wine the Chinese wine waiter (just like a wine waiter in Hector's country except that he was Chinese) was showing him.

Hector asked Édouard to explain what he did in his job, which was 'mergers and acquisitions'. Hector knew a little about it because two pharmaceutical companies, both producing pills prescribed by psychiatrists, had merged. They'd become one big pharmaceutical company with a new name that had no meaning. The funny thing was that, afterwards, the bigger company had done less well than the two smaller companies. Hector had learnt that quite a few people (the ones who read newspapers containing rows of numbers) had lost a lot of money and weren't very happy. At the same time, some of the people who had worked in the two old companies, whom Hector knew because they'd invited him to conferences, had been to see him at his practice. They were very scared or they were very unhappy because, even though the new company now had one name, everyone knew who was from which company and the two groups didn't get on very well, and many of them were afraid of losing their jobs.

Édouard said that this didn't surprise him because mergers often didn't work out very well, the rich people lost money and the not so rich people lost their jobs.

'Why do people keep doing them, then?' asked Hector.

'To keep us in work!' Édouard joked.

He was very pleased to see Hector, and he looked much

more cheerful than at the beginning of the meal.

Édouard also explained that mergers were a bit like his six million dollars: the people who decide them think that they'll be happier afterwards, because they'll be richer or more powerful.

Hector told himself that this dinner was very interesting, that he'd have lots of things to write about happiness, but he was sorry he'd drunk so much wine because his head was going a bit fuzzy.

HECTOR COMES CLOSE TO
HAPPINESS

By the end of the meal, Édouard looked very cheerful indeed, but apparently this wasn't enough for him because he insisted on taking Hector to another place.

'You must get to know China!' he said, although Hector wondered whether the type of places Édouard liked going to, like that restaurant, were the real China. He would have preferred to go back to the hotel and write down what he had learnt about happiness, but since Édouard was his friend he agreed to go where he proposed.

At the entrance was a very tall, very smartly dressed Chinese man wearing an earpiece. When he saw Édouard, he winked at him.

Inside was like a very big bar with soothing music and very soft lighting, and quite a few men like Hector and Édouard — that's to say not only Chinese men. Hector immediately noticed that there were some Chinese women as pretty as the ones in the films, and some of them were so pretty that it almost hurt to look at them. They seemed to be enjoying themselves. They were talking to the men like Hector and Édouard, who also seemed to be enjoying themselves.

Édouard ordered a bottle of white wine, which was placed in an ice bucket on the bar next to them. Almost immediately, a pretty Chinese lady came up to speak to Édouard. They must have known each other quite well because she laughed at all Édouard's jokes and from time to time she whispered things in his ear which made him laugh, too.

This was all very well, but Hector reminded himself that he was making this trip in order to learn about happiness, and he didn't want to forget what he'd discovered during dinner.

He took out his little notebook, opened it on the bar and began writing.

He thought of all those people working very hard so that they could retire one day with six million dollars.

Lesson no. 3: Many people see happiness only in their future.

And then he thought of the people who decided mergers.

Lesson no. 4: Many people think that happiness comes from having more power or more money.

'What are you doing?'

Hector looked up and saw the prettiest Chinese girl he'd ever seen in his life smiling at him.

Hector was quite bowled over, but managed to explain that he was taking notes in order to understand what made people happy or unhappy. The pretty Chinese girl gave a charming little laugh and Hector realised that she thought he was joking. So he began to explain a bit more about why he was taking notes and she stopped laughing and gave him a funny look, but even the funny look she gave him was charming, if you see what I mean.

27

Hector and the very pretty Chinese girl introduced themselves. Her name was Ying Li and she was a student.

'What are you studying?' asked Hector.

'Tourism,' replied Ying Li.

Hector could see why she came here; it was a very good way of getting to know the tourists who visited China. Ying Li asked Hector what he did for a living, and Hector told her about the people who were scared, unhappy or had strange thoughts. Ying Li seemed very interested and said that when she felt sad she went to see her friends and afterwards she felt better. Hector asked her if she'd always lived in this city, and Ying Li began telling him that she came from another part of China where the people were very poor and that she was very happy to be here. She had sisters, but they had stayed behind. Her sisters weren't studying tourism. They worked in the sort of factory Charles had set up in China. Ying Li carried on talking to Hector, because Hector's gift of being genuinely interested in people worked without him even knowing it.

After a while, Édouard tapped him on the shoulder. 'Is everything okay? Are you enjoying yourself?' Hector said that he was and that everything was okay, but he thought that enjoying himself was not at all the right expression: he felt he was in love with Ying Li.

She continued talking about her life, but Hector didn't hear everything she said, because she was so pretty that it was hard for him to look at her and listen at the same time.

Eventually, people began leaving and they left, too. The four of them climbed into a taxi waiting outside: Édouard and his Chinese girlfriend, Ying Li, and Hector, who sat next to the driver. Édouard told the driver where to go in Chinese. They soon arrived outside Hector's hotel, and he realised that he hadn't asked Ying Li for her telephone number. How in God's name would he make sure he saw her again? But he needn't have worried, because Ying Li followed him out of the taxi, and Édouard and his Chinese girl drove off, leaving them standing alone in front of the hotel.

Hector felt a little awkward, but he told himself that a man, even a psychiatrist, should know how to act decisively, and so he took Ying Li by the hand and they walked across the hotel foyer without looking at the staff behind the front desk, and stepped into the lift. And there Ying Li kissed him.

There's no need to say what happened next because, of course, Hector and Ying Li went to Hector's room, where they did what people do when they're in love, and everybody knows what that is.

When Hector woke up the next morning, he heard Ying Li singing in the bathroom. It made him very happy, despite the headache he had as a result of all the wine Édouard had ordered.

Ying Li walked out of the bathroom wrapped in a towel, and when she saw that Hector was awake, she gave another charming little laugh.

Just then the phone rang and Hector answered. It was Édouard, who asked him if he'd had a good evening. Hector said that he had, but it was a little difficult to say any more with Ying Li standing there watching him.

'I chose her for you,' said Édouard, 'I knew you'd like her. Don't worry, it's all taken care of.'

And suddenly Hector understood everything. And he saw

that Ying Li understood that he'd understood, and she stopped smiling and looked a little sad.

Hector was also sad, but he was still nice to Ying Li and gave her a kiss on the cheek when she left, leaving him her telephone number.

He climbed back into bed and after a while he picked up his notebook. He thought for a moment then wrote:

Lesson no. 5: Sometimes happiness is not knowing the whole story.

HECTOR IS UNHAPPY

HECTOR felt very out of sorts that morning. He left his hotel and decided to go and have coffee. He found a huge, very modern café where all they served was coffee, lots of different kinds of coffee. He'd already come across places like that with the same name in almost all the world's big cities where he'd been to conferences, and so he knew how to order in that sort of café, except that this one was full of Chinese men and women talking or reading newspapers, and the waiters and waitresses were also Chinese.

He sat near the window so that he could look out at the street (full of Chinese passers-by, as you've already guessed).

He felt rather unhappy.

But, in reality, being unhappy might also teach him something about happiness. At least it would prove useful for his trip. He began to think: why was he unhappy?

Firstly because he had a headache due to all the wine Édouard had ordered. Hector wasn't used to drinking so much.

Secondly, he was unhappy because of Ying Li.

Ying Li was a simple name, but the reasons why Hector was unhappy were quite complex. He didn't really want to think about it, perhaps because those reasons weren't so easy to accept. It even made him feel a little afraid. He knew this fear only too well, it was what stopped his patients from being able to really think about their problems, and it was his job to help them overcome this fear and really understand what was happening to them.

Just then, the waitress came to ask if he wanted more coffee. She was young and quite pretty; she reminded him of Ying Li and he felt a pang.

Hector opened his notebook and began to draw doodles. This helped him to think. (He would sometimes doodle when his patients kept him on the telephone for too long.)

He was also unhappy because he felt bad when he thought of Clara. Of course she would never know what had happened with Ying Li, but even so he felt bad. On the other hand, if Clara had come with him to China, he would never have met Ying Li. When he was with Clara, Hector always behaved himself, and so he wouldn't have got up to any mischief with Édouard, and so all this was partly Clara's fault. After thinking that, he felt slightly less unhappy.

But there was more. Hector was also unhappy because he hadn't understood what was going on at all. He had thought that Ying Li had approached him because she'd found him interesting with his little notebook, and that later on she'd gone with him to the hotel because she'd found him more and more interesting. But of course that wasn't the reason at all. Ying Li was doing her job, which she probably thought was less tedious than spending her life working like her sisters in one of Charles's factories. When they were still at the bar and Ying Li was telling Hector about herself (of course now he realised that she hadn't told him everything), she'd told him how much her sisters earned in a month: he'd worked out that it was half the price of the bottle of white wine Édouard had ordered, sparkling next to them in its ice bucket.

Hector wasn't sad because he'd discovered how Ying Li earned her living (in fact it did make him a little sad), but because the evening before he'd understood nothing. Or rather, he was sad because that morning he'd understood that he'd understood nothing, because while he still understood nothing he wasn't sad at all, but now that he'd understood that he'd understood nothing he felt sad, if you follow. Realising that one has understood nothing is never pleasant, but for a psychiatrist it's even worse.

The pretty Chinese waitress came back and asked if he wanted more coffee, and when she saw what he was doodling in his notebook she laughed. Hector looked: without knowing it he'd been drawing lots of little hearts.

The waitress went away again and he saw her talking about him to the other waitresses, and they all seemed very amused.

Hector still wasn't in a very good mood, so he paid and left the café.

Outside, he nearly got run over trying to cross the road because he'd forgotten that cars drove on the left in this city. There's no point in looking before crossing the road if you don't look in the right direction.

He wondered what to do with himself. He couldn't see Édouard because he wasn't on holiday; he was working all day at his office. They'd arranged to have dinner again that evening, but Hector wasn't sure he really felt like it any more.

Basically Hector was a little annoyed with Édouard. He knew that Édouard had only wanted to make him happy, but the fact was that this morning Hector was unhappy. Édouard liked drinking a lot, and so Hector had drunk a lot, too. Édouard liked meeting Chinese women whose job it was to make men like him happy, and so Hector had met Ying Li.

Hector told himself that really Édouard was a bit like those friends who are excellent skiers. One day they take you to the top of a very steep ski slope and tell you you'll have great fun if you just follow them. In fact they've only taken you up there because they are excellent skiers and love skiing down very steep slopes. And you don't enjoy yourself at all trying to keep up with them, you're scared, you fall over and you wish it would end, but you have to get down the slope anyway and you have a miserable time while those morons, your friends, fly over the moguls shrieking with joy.

While he was walking, Hector came upon a tiny station with a single track. It wasn't for the usual kind of train but for one of those trains you find in the mountains, because, if you remember, this city was built at the foot of a mountain. And the little train went all the way up to the top of the mountain.

Hector thought that it would do him good to get up into the mountains and so he bought a ticket from an old Chinese man wearing a cap, and he sat down in a tiny wooden carriage.

While he was waiting for the train to move, he began thinking, and he thought about Ying Li again. He could still see her when she'd walked out of the bathroom wrapped in a towel, looking happy; and when she'd stopped smiling because she'd understood that Hector had understood. Afterwards, she'd looked sad and they hadn't known what to say to one another.

The little train moved off and began to climb past the

buildings and very soon it reached the trees and then the clouds, because the weather wasn't good at all, but then the sky turned blue and Hector could see magnificent green mountains all around and, down below, the sea dotted with boats.

It was very beautiful but Hector was still unhappy.

HECTOR COMES CLOSE TO WISDOM

THE station at the top of the mountain was much bigger than the one at the bottom. It was a large concrete cube. Inside were restaurants, souvenir shops and even a wax museum with figures of Tony Blair and Sylvester Stallone. All this was even less like *The Blue Lotus* and this irritated Hector, who was already in quite a bad mood. He left the station and began walking along a road that took him further up the mountain.

The higher he climbed the fewer people he saw. Finally, he was all alone on the road. The surrounding mountains were very beautiful, all green and with quite high peaks. They looked very Chinese. Hector was out of breath, but he felt a lot better.

He stopped to write in his notebook:

Lesson no. 6: Happiness is a long walk in the mountains.

He thought about it then crossed out 'in the mountains' and replaced it with 'in beautiful, unfamiliar mountains'.

At the side of the road he saw a sign in Chinese characters, but fortunately underneath it said in English: 'Tsu Lin Monastery'. Hector was very happy. In monasteries, there are always monks, and maybe in this one he'd find an old monk who would be like Chang's father and who would have interesting things to say about happiness.

The path to the monastery grew steeper and steeper, but Hector didn't feel tired any more because he was eager to arrive. From time to time, at a bend in the road, he would catch a glimpse of the monastery, and it was wonderful, just like in *The Blue Lotus* – the monastery looked really Chinese with its pretty curled rooftop and tiny square windows.

He pulled on a rope and heard a bell ring and a monk came to open the door for him. He was young and looked more like Chang than Chang's father, but his head was shaved and he wore a long orange robe. He spoke very good English and explained to Hector that the monastery was only open to visitors one day a week and that today it was closed. Hector was very disappointed: just when he was beginning to feel better there was some bad news.

And so he persisted; he explained that he'd come a very long way, that he was a psychiatrist and was trying to discover what made people happy or unhappy and he couldn't wait until next week for the monastery to open. The young monk looked uncomfortable, he asked Hector to wait, and left him standing in the little doorway.

There were things for sale which the monks had made, statuettes, pretty saucers, and Hector told himself that he would buy one as a present for Clara.

The young monk came back and Hector was very happy because he'd brought with him an old monk who must have been as old as Chang's father! As soon as he saw Hector, the old monk began laughing, and said: 'Hello. You've come from afar, so I hear.' He said it just like that, no translation was necessary, he spoke Hector's language as well as Hector!

He took Hector into his office, where Hector expected he'd have to kneel on little mats because there'd be no chairs. But it wasn't like that at all. The monk's office looked similar to Hector's, with a proper desk, chairs, a lot of books, a computer, two telephones, statuettes – but Chinese ones – and a splendid view of the mountains.

The old monk explained that in his youth, long before Hector was born, he had spent a few years in Hector's country. He'd been a student, and had earned money washing dishes at a big restaurant where Hector would sometimes have lunch. He asked Hector a lot of questions in order to find out how much things had changed in his country these days, and he seemed very pleased with everything Hector told him.

Hector explained the reason for his trip. More and more of his patients were unhappy without any apparent reason, and he wanted to find out why.

The old monk listened very attentively to Hector, and Hector told himself that he, too, was genuinely interested in people.

Hector asked him whether he had anything interesting to say about happiness.

The old monk said, 'The basic mistake people make is to think that happiness is the goal!' And he began to laugh.

Hector would have liked him to explain this a bit better, but the old monk liked to say things without explaining too much.

And yet, in Hector's country more and more people were turning to the old monk's religion (which wasn't really a religion but it's a bit difficult to explain that here). They thought it would make them happier.

The old monk said that was true, but often people from countries like Hector's didn't really understand his religion, which they adapted to suit themselves – rather like the Chinese restaurants in Hector's city which didn't serve real Chinese food. But the old monk felt that, although in some ways it was a pity, it didn't really matter because it could still help people to be less worried and kinder to others. On the other hand, he wondered why people from Hector's country were so interested in his religion when they had many old and perfectly good religions of their own. Perhaps they'd have been better off taking more of an interest in them; they'd have had a better chance of understanding them properly.

Hector said that it was very complicated, that perhaps people preferred the old monk's religion because there were no bad memories attached to it and therefore it offered hope: people believed that his religion was the one that would really work.

In any event, it seemed to work for the old monk, because Hector had never seen such a contented person who laughed so much, but not in a mocking way. And yet he was very old, and his life couldn't always have been much fun.

Hector remembered that there had been a time when the people who ruled the largest part of China had decided that monks were not useful people, and then some terrible things had happened, things too terrible even to mention. And the old monk came from that part of China, and must have experienced all that, and yet it didn't seem to have stopped him from being happy.

Hector would have very much liked the old monk to reveal the secret of his happiness.

The old monk looked at him, laughing, and said, 'Your journey is a very good idea. When you've reached the end of it, come back and see me.'

HECTOR MAKES A
DISCOVERY

THAT evening, Hector went to wait for Édouard at his office
before going out to dinner. It was Sunday, but Édouard
was at the office because he had to finish a piece of work for the
following day. He was going to show a very important man
how to carry out a merger, and he wanted to do this ahead of
another Édouard from another bank who wanted to show the
same very important man how to do the same thing. And this
very important man in turn wanted to carry out the merger
ahead of another very important man who wanted to do the
same thing. Hector had understood that in business everything
was always a bit of a race whereas in psychiatry it wasn't really
like that, you just had to be careful not to let your patients talk
too much, otherwise you'd be late for the next ones, and they
wouldn't like it.

Hector searched for Édouard's building among the huge
modern towers stretching all the way down to the sea. There
wasn't a beach, only quaysides where huge ships were moored,
or building sites where new towers were going up.

The cars drove underneath, which was convenient as
Hector was able to walk between the tall towers without
any risk of being run over. He arrived at Édouard's very
beautiful, shiny tower. It looked like a giant razor blade. As he
was a little early, he decided to have another coffee, and he

was lucky because there was another big modern glass-walled café.

This time the waitresses weren't very pretty, and Hector was relieved because too much beauty can be exhausting. Indeed, Hector considered being so sensitive to female beauty something of a handicap. And although he knew he wasn't the only one who suffered from it, he hoped that one day he'd get over it. But, as you can see, he hadn't got off to a very good start.

He rang Édouard, who seemed pleased to hear from him, but he hadn't finished working yet. He told Hector to continue waiting for him in the café and he'd meet him there.

Hector began sipping his large coffee and watching the entrance to the tower.

And he saw something he'd seen several times before when he came to this neighbourhood: a group of Chinese women had spread an oilcloth out on the ground and were sitting on it in a circle, like schoolchildren having a picnic. On closer inspection, Hector noticed that they weren't exactly like Chinese women; they were in general slightly shorter, and quite slender and dark-skinned. They seemed to be enjoying themselves, continually chatting and laughing. He'd seen several groups like that when he came to this neighbourhood, with their oilcloths spread out beside the entrance to the towers, under the footbridges or anywhere that gave shelter from the rain, but always outside the buildings.

Hector wondered whether they got together like that in order to practise some new religion. He would have liked to know what it was, perhaps the same one the old monk practised, because, like him, they laughed a lot.

While he was looking out for Édouard, he studied the people coming out of the tower. They were mostly Chinese, but dressed like Édouard at the weekend, in smart polo shirts and deck shoes, and Hector could tell simply from the way they walked that they'd been to the same schools as Édouard, the ones where you learn how to become rich. (Don't forget that Hector is a psychiatrist; he only has to look at people to know where they went to school and whether their grandfather collected butterflies.) There were also westerners like Édouard, and Hector tried to guess where they came from just from the way they looked. No doubt he got it wrong a few times, but since he couldn't check he didn't know, and it amused him, and from time to time he laughed to himself.

Édouard's colleagues didn't look amused at all as they left the towers, they looked tired, and some of them were staring at the ground as if weighed down by worries. When a group of them emerged, talking amongst themselves, they looked very serious and sometimes it seemed as if they were cross with one another. Some looked so preoccupied, so caught up in their own thoughts that Hector almost felt like going up and prescribing pills for them. This café would have been a perfect place to establish himself as a psychiatrist if he had been planning to stay longer.

Finally, he saw Édouard, and he felt glad, because it's always more heartening to see a friend in a foreign country than simply to come across him at home, even if you are slightly annoyed with him. Édouard looked very pleased to see Hector, and he immediately ordered a beer to celebrate.

Hector told Édouard that he looked a lot more cheerful than

all his colleagues whom he'd seen coming out of the tower.

Édouard explained that this was because he was pleased to see Hector, and that Hector should see his face some evenings . . .

'You'd put me straight into hospital!' he said. And he started laughing.

And then he explained that for the past few weeks the markets hadn't been very good and this was why his colleagues weren't very happy.

'So they might lose all their money?' Hector asked.

'No, but they might only get a small bonus, or lose their jobs if the bank downsizes. But at this level you can always find work. You just have to be prepared to go where the jobs are.'

Hector understood that where the jobs were meant other cities with towers that looked like giant razor blades and hotels like those used for conferences.

He asked Édouard who the groups of women were that he'd seen everywhere sitting on their oilcloths. Édouard explained that they were cleaners, and that they all came from the same country, a group of small, very poor islands quite a long way from China. They worked in this city (and other cities in the world) so that they could send money to their families, who'd stayed behind.

'But why do they gather here on those oilcloths?' asked Hector.

'Because they've nowhere else to go,' replied Édouard. 'Today is Sunday, their day off, so they can't stay at work and they don't have enough money to sit in cafés, so they meet here and sit on the ground.'

Édouard also explained that as their country was made up of many small islands, women from particular islands or villages often sat together, and it was almost as if all their oilcloths formed a map of their impoverished archipelago in the midst of these very wealthy towers.

Hector watched the women who had nowhere else to go and who were laughing, he watched Édouard's colleagues coming out of the tower looking very serious and he told himself that the world was a very wonderful or a very terrible place – it was difficult to say which.

When they left the café, Hector wanted to go over and speak to these women, because he felt that it was very important for his investigation. He walked towards a group of them, and as they saw him approach they all stopped talking and smiling. It occurred to Hector that they might think he was going to ask them to move along. But people usually quickly sensed that Hector meant well, and when they heard him speak in English they began laughing again. He told them that he'd been watching them for a while and that they seemed very happy. He wanted to know why.

They looked at one another, chuckling, and then one of them said, 'Because it's our day off!'

And another added, 'Because we're with our friends.'

'Yes, that's right,' the others said, 'it's because we're with our friends.' And even with their families, because some of them were cousins.

Hector asked them what their religion was, and it turned out that it was the same as Hector's! This dated back to the time, long ago, when people of Hector's religion had occupied their islands, because at that time they tended to think that everything belonged to them.

But they didn't seem to hold it against Hector because they all said goodbye to him smiling and waving.

HECTOR ISN'T IN LOVE

Lesson no. 1: Making comparisons can spoil your happiness.

Lesson no. 2: Happiness often comes when least expected.

Lesson no. 3: Many people see happiness only in their future.

Lesson no. 4: Many people think that happiness comes from having more power or more money.

Lesson no. 5: Sometimes happiness is not knowing the whole story.

Lesson no. 6: Happiness is a long walk in beautiful, unfamiliar mountains.

HECTOR reread what he'd written in his notebook. Some of it was interesting, he felt, but even so he wasn't very satisfied. It didn't resemble a proper theory of happiness. (A theory is a story that grown-ups tell each other to explain how things work. People believe it is true until somebody comes up with another theory that explains things better.) In fact, this had given him an idea: at the end of his trip, he would show his list to a famous professor of Happiness Studies.

He had a friend who lived in the country where there are

more psychiatrists than anywhere else in the world, and she knew a professor like that.

Hector was in an Italian restaurant with checked tablecloths and candles on the tables, whose owners, a husband and wife, looked like real Italians. (Actually they'd told Hector that they were Chilean, because even when he was at a restaurant, Hector's apparent interest in people meant that those who came to take his order would first tell him their life story when sometimes all Hector wanted was to order.) It was in the part of the city that was on a hill, where there were still cobbled streets and old houses, and he felt happy to be there.

You must be wondering where Édouard was, but it'll soon become clear.

Hector remembered his visit to the old monk. He wrote:

Lesson no. 7: It's a mistake to think that happiness is the goal.

He wasn't sure whether he'd really understood this lesson, but he thought it was very interesting, and he told himself that at the end of his journey he would go back and see the old monk.

He remembered the women laughing on their oilcloths.

Lesson no. 8: Happiness is being with the people you love.

When he wrote this, his heart started to beat a little faster.

Hector began doodling again.

Because, of course, as you've guessed, Hector was waiting for Ying Li.

When he'd explained to Édouard that he wanted to see Ying Li again, Édouard told him it wouldn't be possible because on Sundays the place full of pretty Chinese girls where they'd met her was closed. But Hector said he didn't want to see Ying Li while she was working. He wanted to invite her to dinner, and since she'd left him her telephone number that was exactly what he was going to do.

And Édouard gave Hector a funny look and said, 'You poor thing!'

Hector got a little annoyed. Édouard shouldn't take him for a fool. He knew perfectly well what Ying Li did for a living! Édouard said that he didn't take Hector for a fool, but he could see that Hector had fallen in love, which was worse than being a fool. He was worried about Hector.

Hector felt reassured, because he realised that Édouard was still a good friend. But he told him that he was mistaken of course; Hector wasn't in love with Ying Li, he simply wanted to see her again. He asked Édouard if he'd ever had a Chinese girlfriend. Édouard said no, not really, but Hector could see that he wasn't quite telling the truth (don't forget that Hector's a psychiatrist). And so Hector said nothing and went 'mmm-hmm' and hoped that Édouard would say more.

But Édouard clearly didn't feel like telling the story of 'not really'. Finally, he said with a sigh, 'The problem over here is that you don't know whether they love you for yourself or for your passport.'

And after a moment he added, 'I'm old enough to ask myself that question, but not so old that I don't care what the answer is.'

And from the way he said it, Hector understood that Édouard had fallen in love and that it can't have ended very happily.

And now Hector was sitting alone at his table in the little Italian restaurant waiting for Ying Li!

When he'd telephoned her she'd sounded a bit surprised, but had immediately accepted his invitation. (It was Édouard who had recommended the restaurant to Hector.)

Now, he was waiting, she was late and he wondered whether she would come. In the meantime he'd ordered a bottle of wine, and he told himself that if he had to wait for her much longer he was going to drink the whole bottle and end up like Édouard.

And then Hector saw Ying Li enter the restaurant, her hair slightly wet from the rain and still so terribly beautiful, and he stood up, knocking over his chair.

The waiters behind the counter practically fell over each other rushing to take Ying Li's coat.

Finally Ying Li sat down opposite Hector and they started talking. But Ying Li was different from the first evening; she seemed almost shy, as though she dared not look at Hector, or was afraid of saying something foolish.

And so Hector began making conversation; he told her a bit about his life, and described the city where he worked. And Ying Li mostly listened, and even told him that she liked his city because it was where they made the things she liked. Indeed, Hector could see that her watch, her belt and her bag were made in his country, although Ying Li had bought them in her city. Hector told himself that this, too, was globalisation. And then he remembered how Ying Li made the money to buy all those very expensive items, and he wondered whether globalisation was such a good thing.

Later, Ying Li dared to say a bit more, though it was clearly difficult for her because there was a subject they both wanted to avoid – her work. And so she spoke about her family.

Her father had taught Chinese history (and being Chinese you can imagine how well he knew his subject). But the people who ruled China when Ying Li was a child had decided that teachers like him were useless, undesirable even, and so he and his family had been sent to the remotest part of China. And there everybody worked in the fields and nobody was allowed to read books except for the one written by the man who ruled China at the time. And that meant Ying Li's sisters never went to school, because the children of undesirable people weren't allowed to study; they had to learn about life from working in the fields. Being younger, Ying Li was later able to catch up a little at school, but then her father had died (he'd never got used to working in the fields and it had worn him out), and she'd been unable to continue her studies.

That was why her sisters, who had never been to school, could only get jobs in Charles's factories. And that was when Ying Li stopped talking, because she realised that now she was going to talk about herself, about why she wasn't a worker like them, and that was rather a delicate subject.

HECTOR FEELS SAD

HECTOR was once again on a plane, and he felt sad. Through the window he could see the sea, so far below that it seemed as if the plane wasn't moving at all.

He had taken out his notebook, but he couldn't think of anything to write.

Sitting next to him was a mother holding her baby – no, it couldn't have been her baby because it had fair hair and blue eyes, like a doll (Hector couldn't tell whether it was a boy or a girl and what's more he didn't really care), and the lady looked like the Asian women he'd seen sitting on their oilcloths. But even though she wasn't the baby's mother, she looked after it very well; she rocked it and spoke to it, and she seemed very fond of it.

Hector was sad because he had the feeling of leaving a place he loved – a city he hadn't even known a week before.

And Édouard had also seemed sad accompanying him to the airport. Clearly he'd thoroughly enjoyed Hector's visit. Édouard had plenty of friends in that city to go out for a drink with, as well as pretty Chinese girls who whispered in his ear, but perhaps not many real friends like Hector.

Of course, he was thinking about Ying Li.

*

In the restaurant, she'd finished telling him about her family and he'd finished telling her about his city, and there'd been a brief silence.

And then Ying Li had said, 'You're kind.'

Hector had been surprised, because he knew that he was fairly kind, but he wondered what Ying Li meant by it. Then she had added, lowering her eyes, 'I'm not used to it.'

And Hector had felt another pang.

They got up from the table and the waiters jostled one another to help Ying Li on with her coat.

They found themselves outside in the tiny cobbled street.

Hector, of course, very much wanted to take Ying Li back to his hotel, but he felt awkward because that was exactly what the men she worked with did. He sensed that Ying Li also felt awkward, even though she wanted to stay with him.

And so they entered a bar at random, and it was most bizarre in there; there weren't many people, only some Chinese men who all seemed to know each other and were taking turns to get up on a stage and sing songs in Chinese, probably famous songs. Hector even recognised a Charles Trenet tune, but not the words. And the Chinese men were laughing and buying rounds of drinks. They seemed just like the people in Hector's country, and he remembered what Charles had said on the plane: the Chinese aren't really any different from us.

It even made Ying Li laugh, and Hector was glad to see her so cheerful. And when Ying Li laughed he could see how young she was, despite all the expensive things she was wearing that evening.

But it probably wasn't a good idea to have gone into that bar because, as Hector and Ying Li were leaving, a big car pulled up beside them.

And the tall Chinese man from the other night, the one with the earpiece, stepped out, and in the back Hector could see a not very young Chinese lady looking angrily at Ying Li. The tall Chinese man didn't even look at Hector, he spoke to Ying Li, and she answered him nervously. Hector couldn't understand what they were saying because they were speaking Chinese, but he could see that the Chinese man was questioning Ying Li in an unfriendly voice, and that she was flustered. And so Hector put on the foolish air of a satisfied client who understands nothing, and asked the Chinese man in English, 'Should I pay you?'

The tall Chinese man was a little taken aback but he calmed down. He even smiled at Ying Li, although it wasn't a pleasant smile. He told Hector that there was no need, that he could just pay Ying Li. And he climbed back into his big car and put his foot flat on the accelerator and sped off. But Hector didn't see that, because Ying Li was already crying in his arms.

Afterwards, it was easier to take her back to the hotel in a taxi, because a man consoling a woman who was crying didn't have much to do with Ying Li's work, it had more to do with Hector's.

And then in the room, Ying Li stopped crying and they lay on the bed in the dark, although the room was lit up faintly by the city lights outside, and Ying Li remained motionless in Hector's arms.

He was prepared to lie next to her all night if necessary, but Ying Li soon showed him that she wanted to do what people in love do.

It was different from the first night, it was less joyful, but far more intense.

The next morning when Hector woke up, Ying Li had gone without leaving a note or anything. Hector had wanted to give her money, because he was thinking about the Chinese man, but he realised that Ying Li must have preferred to arrange things herself.

Hector wanted to talk to Édouard immediately, and they met at the café at the bottom of the tower, and because it was Monday it was full of people. Édouard listened to Hector, very seriously, the way Hector listened to people when they told him their story. And then he said, 'They won't take it out on her, she's too valuable. And anyway, I know the Chinese man. I'll sort it all out. But as far as you two are concerned I don't think it would be a very good idea for you to see each other again.'

Hector had thought the same, but it's one thing thinking something and another thing knowing it, and Édouard said, 'You poor thing . . .'

And now, on the plane, Hector couldn't think of anything to write in his notebook.

The baby had been looking at him for a while, and stretching its arms out towards him. This made the nanny laugh – because of course you've guessed that she was the nanny – and the baby as well.

So Hector smiled at them and felt a little less sad.

Suddenly, a tall blonde lady came up and stood in the aisle near them. Hector understood that this was the mother, who was no doubt travelling with her husband in business class.

'Is everything all right?' she asked the nanny.

And then she left again. And the baby's face crumpled and it began screaming.

Hector took his notebook and wrote down:

Lesson no. 8b: Unhappiness is being separated from the people you love.

HECTOR MEETS UP WITH
A GOOD FRIEND

HECTOR was on yet another plane, but this one was rather different from all the others.

(Between this plane and the one before there'd been another, and then another, but these weren't mentioned because, besides thinking about Ying Li and Clara, nothing much had happened to Hector.)

Firstly, this plane was full of African men and women. Hector was practically the only white person on the plane. Many of the men and women were smartly dressed, almost as if they came from another era, like Hector's grandparents in the country, when they went to mass. The women had on long flowery dresses and the men rather baggy suits. Another thing that reminded him of the country was their huge shopping bags, and some even had live chickens and ducks in cages! These animals were quite noisy, but that was just as well because they drowned out the noise of the plane, which also dated from another era. Hector remembered the patients who came to see him because they were afraid of flying, and he told himself that after this flight he'd understand them a lot better. On the other hand, if the plane was old, it was because it had never crashed, which was somewhat reassuring.

Sitting next to him was an African lady with her baby. This time it wasn't a nanny, but the baby's real mother. She rocked her child as she read. The baby looked at Hector, who was looking at the lady's book. Lady isn't really the right word because she was quite young, about Hector's age. And you'll never guess: the book she was reading was a book on psychiatry! The lady was a psychiatrist!

They both found it funny to be sitting next to a colleague, and the lady, whose name was Marie-Louise, explained that she was going back to her country on holiday, because in fact she worked in the country they had just taken off from, where there are more psychiatrists than anywhere else in the world. Hector felt nervous about asking her why she hadn't stayed in her own country (a little like when he asked Charles why he hadn't built his factories in his own country, if you remember), but the lady was quick to explain why.

'I want my children to live a normal life.'

She had two older children who had stayed at home, and Hector asked her what she called a normal life. (Even psychiatrists can ask each other questions.)

Marie-Louise replied, 'I want them to be able to go to school without needing a driver and a bodyguard, for example.'

Hector agreed that indeed that wasn't a normal life, even though, when he was a child, he would have been very proud to go to school with a driver and a bodyguard, but mothers don't think like that, of course.

And then the plane began to tilt to one side and make a noise like the dive-bombers in documentaries about the war, and everybody went quiet, except for the chickens and ducks, which made more noise than ever.

Fortunately, this didn't go on for very long and the plane

finally landed quite normally, though with a lot of juddering.

Hector managed to let go of the armrests, and when all the passengers were standing in the aisle, Marie-Louise invited him to come and visit her and her family. She wrote down her address in his little notebook.

When he reached the door to the plane, Hector had exactly the same sensation as when you open the oven to see whether the roast beef is ready and the oven is very hot. This was slightly different though, because it was very bright outside and the sun was beating down. The airport was surrounded by scorched-looking mountains, a bit like the colour of overdone roast beef as a matter of fact.

At customs, the customs officers were African (but we won't repeat this all the time, like with the Chinese; in this country everybody is African, apart from a few exceptions, which we'll point out). Families waited in the shade. The little girls were dressed in white ankle socks and ruffs and the little boys in shorts, well, long shorts actually, like the ones worn in Hector's country a long time ago.

Hector couldn't see the friend who was supposed to be meeting him. And so he walked out carrying his suitcase, and the sun kept beating down. A porter soon arrived to help him carry his suitcase over to the taxi rank, which was a few yards away, and then another and another, and Hector thought they were going to start fighting, but fortunately he saw his friend Jean-Michel coming towards him, smiling.

Jean-Michel was an old friend of Hector's, like Édouard, although they were quite different. Jean-Michel had studied medicine. He had specialised in the germs that make people sick in hot countries. And although they had plenty of these germs, unfortunately hot countries also had the fewest doctors. So Jean-Michel had quickly gone off to work in these countries. He was tall and strong, and looked a bit like a sailing or skiing instructor. Hector remembered that he'd been popular with the girls but that he'd never seemed very interested in them, and so they became even more interested in him and often came and asked Hector about Jean-Michel because they knew the two of them were friends.

Jean-Michel took Hector's suitcase, and they walked towards the car park. This sounds simple, but in fact it was rather complicated because there were beggars in the car park. They'd immediately noticed Hector, just like the porters had before. And soon, all the beggars in the car park surrounded Hector, stretching out their hands and saying, 'Monsieur, monsieur, monsieur, monsieur, monsieur . . .'

Hector could see that some of them were very ill, very thin, and some only had one eye. They seemed barely able to stand up, but they continued to surround him like ghosts, holding out their hands.

Jean-Michel strode ahead, and appeared not even to see the beggars. He carried on talking to Hector.

'I've found you a good hotel . . . Well, it wasn't difficult, there are only two.'

By the time they reached the car, Hector had already given away all his coins and even his bank notes, and it was only then that Jean-Michel noticed what was going on.

'Ah yes, of course,' he said, 'it's your first time here.'

Jean-Michel's car was a big white four-wheel-drive vehicle

with letters painted on it. Next to it, a young African man with a pump-action shotgun stood waiting for them.

'This is Marcel,' said Jean-Michel, 'he's our bodyguard.'

The car left the car park and took the road into the city. Through the window, Hector again saw the scorched mountains, the beggars who were watching them drive away, the sun beating on the potholed road and then, sitting in front of him, Marcel with his pump-action shotgun resting on his knees. He told himself that in this country he was perhaps going to reach a better understanding of happiness, but no doubt with quite a few lessons in unhappiness, too.

HECTOR DOES A GOOD
TURN

THE hotel was very pretty. The grounds were large and full of flowering trees and small bungalows for the guests, and there was a big wiggly-shaped swimming pool, which even passed under a tiny wooden footbridge. But it felt a little different from the kind of hotel people go to on holiday. First of all, at the entrance there was a sign saying: 'We kindly request our guests and their visitors not to bring weapons into the hotel. Please go to reception.' And inside the hotel there were white men in uniforms (a funny-looking uniform with shorts) drinking at the bar. They belonged to a sort of small army, which all the countries in the world had formed to bring some order to this country. But since this country wasn't very important, nobody had wanted to pay much money towards the small army, and so it was scarcely big enough to defend itself and didn't manage to bring much order even though it tried.

A man at the bar explained all of this to Hector. He was white, but he wasn't wearing a uniform; he wore the kind of clothes Édouard wore at the weekend: a nice, light-coloured shirt, well-pressed trousers and what looked like golf shoes, and a watch that must have cost as much as Ying Li's. (These days, lots of things made Hector think of Ying Li.)

The man was a foreigner, but he spoke Hector's language very well and only drank sparkling water. And funnily enough, he had almost the same name as Édouard; he was called Eduardo! Hector asked him what country he came from and Eduardo told him. It was a country that didn't have a very good reputation, because almost everywhere there people grew a plant, which was made into a very harmful stimulant, which was illegal in Hector's country, and in every country in the world for that matter. As a result, many people were prepared to pay a lot of money for it. Of course, it wasn't Eduardo's fault that he was born in that country, and so Hector did not think much of it. He asked Eduardo where he'd learnt to speak his language so well.

'In your country! I spent several years there.'

Eduardo sounded as if he didn't want to say any more about it. And so to change the subject, Hector asked him what he was doing here in this country. Eduardo looked at Hector, and because, as previously mentioned, people sensed that Hector meant well – particularly clever people like Eduardo – he replied with a chuckle, 'Farming!'

Hector thought that this was interesting for his investigation. He asked Eduardo what made him happy in life. Eduardo reflected for a moment and said, 'Seeing my family happy, knowing that my children won't want for anything.'

Eduardo's children were grown up, and he hoped to send them to study in the big country that had more psychiatrists than anywhere else in the world. Hector asked him whether it bothered him to know that other families might be very unhappy because their children took the harmful stimulant Eduardo made (because, of course, you, like Hector, have worked it out by now).

This time Eduardo answered straight away.

'If they take it, it's because their family's already messed up. Their parents don't look after them properly, all they think about is making money, or getting laid. It's normal for kids to go off the rails!'

'Okay,' said Hector.

He didn't necessarily think that it was okay, but when a psychiatrist says 'okay', it just means 'I understand what you're saying.' But he pointed out to Eduardo that lots of poor people also took this harmful drug and it made their lives even worse. Eduardo said that it was the same thing: their whole country was like a bad family which didn't look after its children properly.

'I don't create demand,' said Eduardo, 'I simply respond to it.'

Hector said that he understood, but all the same he thought that Eduardo was building his and his family's happiness on other people's misery. But he told himself that Eduardo had also been born in a country that was like one big very bad family. And so naturally he had a strange way of looking at things.

For that matter, Hector's questions might have annoyed Eduardo a bit, because he ordered a whisky from the African barman, who came over and served him. You might be thinking that not enough has been said about African people in a country where everybody is African, but the reason is that the only African people in the bar were the waiters, the barman and the receptionist, and they didn't talk at all. The people talking were the white people, guests like Eduardo and Hector, and the men in shorts.

When Hector told Eduardo that he was a psychiatrist, he seemed very interested. He told him that his wife was always unhappy (and yet she didn't want for anything). And so the doctor over in his country had tried prescribing various pills, but none of them had really worked. What did Hector think?

Hector asked for the names of the pills. Eduardo said that he had the names in his room, and he went to fetch them. In the meantime, Hector drank his whisky (because Eduardo had ordered one for him as well) and began talking to the barman. His name was Isidore. Hector asked him what made him happy. Isidore smiled and said, 'My family not wanting for anything.'

Hector asked if that was all.

Isidore thought about it, and then added, 'Going to my second job from time to time!'

Hector understood that besides his job as a barman Isidore had another job, which he must really enjoy. What sort of job was it? Isidore started to laugh and was about to explain to Hector, but Eduardo came back with his wife's prescription.

Hector studied it, and found that the prescription was not quite right. The psychiatrist over there had prescribed all three main types of medication psychiatrists prescribe, but none of them in the right dose, so they couldn't have been helping Eduardo's wife much. He asked Eduardo a few more questions in order to find out what sort of unhappiness his wife was suffering from, and he soon saw which type of pill would work best for her. He also remembered a good psychiatrist from Eduardo's country whom he'd met at a conference. It was understandable that Eduardo hadn't heard of him, because this psychiatrist worked at a hospital, and he wore socks with his sandals, whereas people like Eduardo tend to know doctors who wear the same type of shoes as they do. Hector gave Eduardo his name and also the name of the pill that his wife should try while she was waiting for an appointment. Eduardo wrote everything down with a nice gold pen (it might even have been solid gold).

Just then, Jean-Michel arrived and when he saw Hector talking to Eduardo, he pulled a face. Hector wanted to introduce Jean-Michel to Eduardo, but Jean-Michel seemed in a hurry and he whisked Hector away while Eduardo thanked him and said goodbye.

In the car, Jean-Michel asked Hector if he knew who he'd been speaking to.

Hector said he did, more or less.

And Jean-Michel said, 'That's the kind of guy who drags this country into the shit!'

Marcel said nothing, but it was obvious he agreed.

Hector didn't reply because he was busy writing in his notebook:

Lesson no. 9: Happiness is knowing your family lacks for nothing.

Lesson no. 10: Happiness is doing a job you love.

He explained to Jean-Michel that the barman at the hotel had a second job. This made Jean-Michel and Marcel laugh, and Marcel explained that here having a second job meant having a girlfriend as well as a wife!

This made Hector think about Ying Li and Clara, and he went very quiet for a while.

HECTOR TAKES LESSONS IN UNHAPPINESS

THERE were a lot of people walking along the dusty street, and some little children with no shoes on as well, and when the car got stuck in traffic, the children came up to beg. They'd spotted Hector even through the tinted windows, and they waved their little hands at him and smiled, showing all their little white teeth.

'Don't try to wind the window down,' Jean-Michel said, 'I've locked them.'

'But why are they only making signs at me?' Hector asked, as he watched a pretty little girl holding out her pretty little hands.

'Because they can see that you're new here. They already know us.'

The city did not look very well maintained. Hector could see tumbledown houses patched up with planks of wood or corrugated iron, or villas that must once have been very beautiful but were now mouldering. People were selling things on the pavement, but they were the sorts of things that, in Hector's country, would just have been thrown away or put up in the attic. One place, however, was selling nice brightly coloured vegetables. Hector noticed that the people did not look very happy. The children smiled, but the grown-ups didn't smile at all.

They were still stuck in traffic, and Hector couldn't understand why there were so many cars in such a poor country.

'There aren't that many cars, it's just that there are very few roads so they get congested quickly. And there's only one set of traffic lights in the whole city!'

Finally, they managed to get out of the traffic jam and the car was soon speeding along the road. The road wasn't very well maintained either; it had big boulders in the middle or else potholes the size of bathtubs, which nobody bothered to fill in, but Jean-Michel was used to it. This was just as well, because from time to time they went past trucks driving very fast the other way with lots of people clinging to the sides and even on the roof. Hector told himself that people here might not smile very much, but in any event they seemed to know no fear, because had any of those trucks had an accident they would have been very badly hurt. Hector noticed that the trucks were often painted different colours and had writing on them in big letters: 'The Good Lord watches over us' or 'Long live Jesus who loves us always' and he understood that the people here still put their trust in God, much more so than in Hector's country where people relied on the Social Security to look after them.

He wondered whether belief in God was a lesson in happiness. No, he couldn't make that a lesson because you don't choose whether to believe in God or not.

The countryside wasn't much better than it had been around the airport: big scorched hills and hardly any trees to provide shade.

Hector asked why there were so few trees in this country.

This time it was Marcel who explained. It was because of the embargo. This country had for a long time been run by quite bad people, but one day even worse people took over, which ended up by annoying countries like Hector's. And so the presidents and prime ministers of those countries had got together and voted for an embargo to force the bad people to resign. An embargo is when a country isn't allowed to buy from or sell to other countries, so that it becomes even poorer, and the inhabitants get angry and this forces their country's leaders to behave properly or resign. The problem is that it never works, because in general the leaders of those countries couldn't care less if their people starve, even the babies, whereas the people who voted for the embargo come from countries where people and babies are looked after, and they can't understand it, and so the embargo continues and the babies grow thinner and their mothers are very sad.

It hadn't been good for the trees either, because since the country was unable to buy oil or gas due to the embargo, people living in towns had had to go and cut wood in order to build fires to do their cooking. As a result, in many places there were no more trees. And this meant that the rain had washed away the soil and all that was left was big hills of rock, and rocks aren't much use unless you like collecting them.

'And now,' Marcel said, 'the United Nations wants to finance a reforestation project, but have you ever seen trees growing out of rock?'

Marcel didn't look very happy as he was saying all this; he seemed a little angry at the United Nations (the people who had voted for the embargo), even though the bad people who'd been running the country had finally gone. But, if the bad people had gone, why did it seem as if things were not getting better? Marcel explained that the people here had elected a president who was a good man and had always been against the bad people who were there before, but that as soon as he became leader himself he'd become a bit like them.

Finally the road began to climb, and they came to a prettier area with trees and small villages, and Hector noticed that the people he saw along the roadside looked happier, and when the car slowed down to pass a donkey or a cart, the children didn't come up to beg.

They stopped in front of a building next to a small church. Above it was written 'Health Centre' and outside on a bench in the shade lots of African women were waiting with their babies.

They smiled at Hector when they saw him go in with Jean-Michel, and Jean-Michel explained that they must think that Hector was a new doctor, which wasn't entirely untrue after all, because, contrary to what some people say, psychiatrists are real doctors!

Inside there were some other young African women in white coats examining babies, and a young man, too. They looked very pleased to see Jean-Michel and Hector arrive. Jean-Michel explained that they were all nurses, but that they did a lot of the same things that doctors in Hector's country do, and that he only went there to see children who had slightly more complicated illnesses. Because after going there, Jean-Michel had three more health centres to visit.

Hector left him to work and went outside to find Marcel

smoking a pipe in the shade of the trees. He asked Marcel why people seemed happier here than in the city.

'In the country you can always get by with a bit of land and some chickens. And families stay together, people support each other. In the city people can't manage without money. And families crack under the strain, and there's a lot of alcohol and drugs, and people see what they could buy if they only had the money. There aren't as many temptations here.'

Hector told himself that this reminded him of at least three of the lessons he'd already written down.

But he had also learnt another:

Lesson no. 11: Happiness is having a home and a garden of your own.

He thought about everything he'd seen and heard since his arrival and wrote:

Lesson no. 12: It's harder to be happy in a country run by bad people.

And this reminded him of the old Chinese monk's life and the story of Ying Li's family. And a little of Ying Li, too, of course.

HECTOR LEARNS ANOTHER
LESSON

Dusk was falling and they were on their way back to the city, because Jean-Michel said that it was better not to drive at night in this country,

You may have been wondering why Marcel was sitting in the car with a pump-action shotgun on his knees acting as a bodyguard. Why would anyone want to harm Jean-Michel who went all over the place trying to cure babies?

Here's why. In this country a car was a highly prized object and it's difficult to start modern cars without the ignition key. So here, criminals waited at places where you had to stop (not at traffic lights, as there was only one, but where a boulder was blocking the road for example), and then they came with their revolvers and made you get out of the car and they drove off with the car and the keys. The problem was that before stealing the car they would often kill the people inside because they didn't want to be reported or simply because they were nervous, had drunk too much rum or beer or had taken harmful drugs.

'It's happening more and more,' said Jean-Michel. 'Every day criminals arrive from elsewhere because the police are less efficient here than in their own countries, and it's easier not to get caught.'

'It's globalisation,' said Marcel, laughing.

Police inefficiency was also the reason why people like

Eduardo came here to do business, and, what's more, it was often the police they came to do business with; it was more practical that way.

At the hotel bar, there were still some uniformed men in shorts, but not Eduardo, which was just as well because Hector sensed that Jean-Michel and Eduardo weren't made to get on together.

Isidore, the barman who had a second job, looked pleased to see Hector again. He immediately served them a beer, which Hector thought was excellent, because in this country where nothing worked properly they still produced excellent beer.

Hector asked Jean-Michel if he was happy. This made Jean-Michel laugh. (Hector reflected later that this question tended to make men laugh but sometimes made women cry.)

'I never ask myself that question, but I think I am. I do a job that I love, and that I know I do well, and, on top of that, I feel really useful over here. And as you've seen, I get on with the people here. We're a real team.'

Jean-Michel drank some beer and then said, 'Every day here has meaning.'

Hector found this very interesting because he also had a useful profession in his country, though sometimes, when all he saw were people who were unhappy for no apparent reason with no real disorders and whom he found it difficult to help, he wondered whether his life had any meaning, and that didn't make him very happy.

'Also,' Jean-Michel said, 'I feel loved for who I am.'

And perhaps by now you've realised that Jean-Michel and

Marcel were more than just friends, or more than just a doctor and his bodyguard, and you've also understood why Jean-Michel was never very interested in girls. But he'd never talked to Hector about this before, and he didn't really talk about it now, since there's no need to explain everything to a friend who's a psychiatrist (or to a friend who isn't a psychiatrist for that matter).

Hector noticed that Jean-Michel glanced at him to see how he'd taken it, and that he was looking a little nervous. And so Hector said, 'It's true. I don't think I've ever seen you so happy.'

And then Jean-Michel smiled, and ordered two more beers, and they didn't mention it again, because that's the way men are.

Jean-Michel left and Hector went to his room to lie down for a bit before dinner. That evening he was going to the house of Marie-Louise, the fellow psychiatrist he'd met on the plane who'd invited him to meet her family.

His room was very nice if you like that sort of thing, with marble flooring and furniture of the kind you'd find at a château, except newer, and a red bathtub with gilt taps. Hector was resting on the bed when the telephone rang.

It was Clara. Hector had left her a message during the day, because she'd been in a meeting.

'Are you enjoying yourself?' she asked Hector.

This made Hector feel bad because it was the same question Édouard had whispered in his ear when he was speaking to Ying Li for the first time in the bar with soft lighting.

'Yes, it's very interesting.'

But at the same time, Hector felt awkward because of course he couldn't tell her the most interesting thing. This was the first time he really felt that he was deceiving Clara.

'And how about you? How are things at work?'

'Oh, not bad, we had a good meeting.'

Clara explained that the name she'd chosen for the new pill had been approved by the directors. It was a triumph for her. Hector congratulated her.

It was all a bit flat. They continued to talk but as if they didn't really have anything important or exciting to say and were just being polite. Finally they said goodbye and sent each other a kiss.

Hector fell back on the bed, and his head started to swim.

He'd just understood why he couldn't forget Ying Li.

It wasn't because she was very pretty, since Clara was pretty too. (Hector had often had pretty girlfriends – perhaps because he wasn't very happy with his own physique and so he felt that being with a pretty girlfriend balanced that out.)

It wasn't because he'd done with Ying Li what people in love do and it had been very intense, because frankly Hector had enough experience of that sort of thing not to fall in love so easily.

No, he was remembering the moment when he'd really fallen in love with Ying Li.

Perhaps you worked it out before he did, because, in matters of love, psychiatrists aren't necessarily more intelligent than anyone else.

It was when Ying Li came out of the bathroom all happy and then suddenly became sad, when she understood that Hector had just understood.

It was when they had dinner together and Hector sensed that she was intimidated.

It was when she cried in his arms.

It was each time she was moved when she was with him.

Hector had fallen in love with Ying Li's emotions, and that was a very profound feeling indeed.

HECTOR LEARNS WHY
CHILDREN SMILE

'HELP yourself to some more goat and sweet potato stew,' said Marie-Louise.

And Hector did because it was very good. No wonder the wolf was so keen to eat the goat in Aesop's fable, he said to himself.

There were a lot of people at the table: Marie-Louise's mother, a tall, rather mournful lady; Marie-Louise's sister and her husband; one of Marie-Louise's younger brothers, and various cousins and friends, he wasn't quite sure. The funny thing was that none of them were the same colour: Marie-Louise's mother's skin looked like Hector's when he was tanned, her sister was darker, and the cousins were all different, the younger brother was dark like Marcel, and they were all extremely nice to Hector. On a sideboard stood a photograph of a handsome man in a smart suit. It was Marie-Louise's father. She had told Hector that he had been a lawyer, and that many years ago, when the bad people were in power, as they usually were in this country, he had wanted to get into politics. One morning, when Marie-Louise was still a little girl, he had kissed her goodbye and left for the office, and in the evening a truck had dumped him in front of the house and driven away quickly. Her father was dead and had been badly beaten. Politics was often like that in this country. Marie-Louise seemed used to telling the story after all that time, but after she'd finished Hector had a lump in his throat.

'My mother's never got over it,' she explained. 'I think she's still depressed.'

And, looking at Marie-Louise's mother sitting silently at one end of the table, Hector could see very well that it was true.

Hector and Marie-Louise began to discuss pills and psychotherapy. Marie-Louise had tried absolutely everything, including taking her mother to be treated in the big country where she worked that had so many psychiatrists, but her mother had never really come back to life. Because there are some tragedies in life which psychiatry can help, but not cure.

Marie-Louise's sister's husband, Nestor, was quite an amusing sort who enjoyed joking with Hector, and was in business. At first, Hector was worried that he might be in the same business as Eduardo, but he wasn't. Nestor imported cars and exported paintings by local artists (painting was the other excellent thing in this country besides beer). He also owned a factory where people made shoes so that people in Hector's country could go jogging. (Looking at Nestor, Hector thought that there were certainly Charleses of every hue in this world.) Hector asked him whether this helped people here to become less poor. Nestor said that it helped a little, but that it would take hundreds like him.

'The problem is that this country is unstable. And so businessmen don't want to risk their money here, there's no investment, and therefore no jobs. People talk about globalisation, but the problem is that we're not part of it!'

Hector understood that, contrary to what some people in his

country believed, globalisation wasn't always a bad thing.

Marie-Louise's husband wasn't there. He'd been born in this country, but worked as an engineer now in the big country that had so many psychiatrists, which wasn't much help to his country, except that he sent money to his family who were still here. This was all because Marie-Louise didn't want her children to have to go to school with a bodyguard.

Hector had a question he wanted to ask about children. Why did the children he'd seen in the city smile all the time, even though they lived in the street and had nothing, no shoes, and often no parents to look after them? The grown-ups didn't smile, which was understandable given the lives they had. But why did the little children seem happy?

Everybody thought the question was very interesting. They came up with lots of answers.

'Because they don't yet fully realise their situation, they can't make comparisons.'

This reminded Hector of lesson no. 1.

'Because children who are sad die more quickly, so we don't see them. Only happy children survive.'

'Because they were pleased to see Hector.'

Everybody burst out laughing, and Marie-Louise told Hector that this proved it was true!

And then one of the cousins (she was rather too pretty, so Hector had been careful not to look at her too much) said, 'Because they know that people will be kinder to a child who smiles.'

Everybody thought that this was the best explanation, and Marie-Louise's cousin looked at Hector and smiled, and he wondered whether it wasn't because she wanted him to be nice to her, but fortunately the whole family was there to stop them from getting up to any mischief.

This question of children smiling reminded Hector of the story of one of his fellow psychiatrists. When he was a child, people from another country had occupied Hector's country and had decided to put to death all the people with surnames they didn't like. In order to do this they put them on trains and took them very far away, to places where nobody could see them doing this terrible thing. Hector's colleague was a child with the wrong sort of surname, and he'd been kept in a camp with other children waiting for the train that would take them to their deaths. But because he was a child who smiled and made everybody laugh, including the people guarding the camp, some of the grown-ups had kept him back, hidden him, and he hadn't been taken away with the others.

This was something all children wanting to survive should know, then: people are kinder to a child who smiles, even if it doesn't always work.

It was getting late, and because the food had been spicy and made Hector thirsty, he'd drunk quite a lot and was feeling rather drowsy. Everybody said goodbye, and Marie-Louise went with Hector to the car that had come to take him back to the hotel. It was a small four-by-four truck like Jean-Michel's, with a chauffeur – not dressed like the chauffeurs in Hector's country, though; he just wore a T-shirt, a pair of old bell-bottoms and some flip-flops. There was also a very young bodyguard carrying a very big revolver. When he walked past them to climb into the back, he could smell that they'd been drinking rum, but all things considered maybe it was a good way of not being scared when driving on the roads in that country. He waved goodbye to Marie-Louise and her family, who stood on the front step watching him leave, and the car drove off into the night.

Hector felt quite happy: he told himself that he would have plenty of interesting things to tell Clara, because he would be able to tell her about what happened to him in this country.

He would have liked to talk to the chauffeur and the bodyguard, to ask them if they were happy, but he was too drowsy. He fell asleep.

He dreamt about Ying Li, which proves that psychiatrists' dreams are no more difficult to understand than anybody else's.

HECTOR'S LIFE IS NO
LONGER PEACEFUL

H<small>E</small> didn't wake up completely but he did have the fleeting impression that the car had stopped, the doors had slammed and people had started shouting. However, because he was dreaming that he was sailing across the sea in a small boat with Ying Li to go back to his country, he resisted coming out of his dream.

Well, that was a big mistake.

Because when Hector did wake up completely, he had the impression that the driver and the bodyguard had changed. True, Hector had not paid much attention to what they looked like but he could see perfectly well that these were not the same men as before, and he tried to understand why. The other thing he tried to understand was why the car was still driving through the night. Because his hotel wasn't all that far from Marie-Louise's house, just about time enough for one dream, and yet they were still on the road.

If Hector had been more awake, or a bit smarter (Hector was intelligent but not necessarily smart), he would have guessed what was happening, but instead he asked, 'Where are we going?'

The two Africans in front jumped out of their seats, nearly hitting their heads on the roof, and the car swerved sharply. They turned around, the whites of their eyes showing, and the one driving said, 'Mercy!' The other one took out a big revolver and pointed it shakily at Hector. At that moment, Hector saw that they were both wearing police uniforms. Then he understood what had happened.

It was as Marcel had explained. Stealing a car is difficult without the ignition key, and so it's easier for criminals to make you stop and give them your keys. In this country, some criminals had discovered that a good way of doing this was to pretend to be policemen! Obviously, when a policeman flags you down on the road you stop, otherwise you risk getting fined or even being shot at. So, at night, sometimes there were fake police roadblocks or, rather, real roadblocks but manned by fake policemen who were actually criminals. And it wasn't that difficult to get hold of uniforms because everybody had a brother or a cousin in the police force who could lend them his jacket or helmet on his days off (the jacket was enough because in this country even the real policemen could wear just any old trousers or shoes, even battered trainers).

Hector understood everything. The two fake policemen in front must have stopped the car, posing as real policemen, made the driver and the bodyguard get out, perhaps roughed them up a bit, and then left in a hurry without even realising that Hector was asleep in the back.

As he looked at the gun pointing at him, Hector began to feel scared, but not very scared. He knew that some men, especially criminals, could be very cruel or very scared and kill people, but since he'd never witnessed this at first hand (Hector had led quite a peaceful life, like most people his age in his country), he couldn't really believe that anybody was going to hurt him, even though he knew it was possible.

Meanwhile, the man in the bodyguard's seat had begun talking very fast into a mobile phone. Hector couldn't understand everything because he was speaking in a language that was similar to Hector's but not identical; it was a local version of it, which dated back to the time, long ago, when the people in Hector's country thought that this country belonged to them. Judging by his tone of voice, Hector understood that he was talking to his boss, and that his boss wanted Hector brought to him. This didn't seem like such a bad thing, because, as his mother would say (and perhaps yours too), it is always better to speak to the Good Lord directly than to one of his saints.

Although later, on seeing the boss, he wondered whether his mother was always right.

The boss looked at Hector without saying anything, as you might look at a chair or an unwanted parcel you don't know how to dispose of, while the other two explained what had happened in voices a little high-pitched for two such burly men. You'll have realised that they were scared of their boss – and since they were criminals, this gives you some idea of what their boss must have been like; he can't have been easy-going, any more than his two friends who were with him at the table when they arrived.

They were in a big house, which must have been splendid once but was in ruins now. Hector could see through into another room where some beautiful African women were sitting on a big sofa watching television. They all wore pretty, rather tight-fitting dresses and earrings, and looked as if they'd just come from the hairdresser's. From time to time one of them would get up with a sigh and come to the door to take a peek at

Hector or to listen to what the others were saying, but Hector avoided looking at her, because now really wasn't the time for fun and games.

The boss was better dressed than his men, and he spoke Hector's language without a trace of the local accent, and Hector guessed that he was the type of criminal Marcel had told him about who had come here because the police weren't very efficient.

One of the boss's friends at the table said, 'We're in the shit now because of these two idiots!'

And the other friend scowled at Hector and muttered, 'What are you staring at?'

Hector began to explain; he told them he'd been to dinner with Marie-Louise's family. The others looked at each other, and then the one who'd said 'What are you staring at?' said, 'That's all we need!' Hector also explained that he was a doctor (he didn't dare tell them that he was a psychiatrist; he wasn't sure why but he thought it might annoy the boss of the gang) and that he was a friend of Jean-Michel, the doctor who treated the children at the health centres.

But he didn't have time to say much more, because the boss ordered the others to take him away and he found himself locked in a kind of storeroom with a small light bulb on the ceiling and lots of beer crates. It also smelt very strongly of dead rat, and the smell gave Hector a bad feeling.

The door wasn't very thick and he could hear what they were saying.

The criminals couldn't agree, and it sounded as if they were squabbling. It was difficult to follow, but it went a bit like this:

One kept saying, 'How much could we get for him?'

Another always replied, 'Forget it, he's white, we'll never get away with it.'

And so the first insisted, 'Exactly, he's worth a lot because he's white.'

But the third kept repeating, 'In any case, he's seen us now.'

Hector had the impression that it was the boss who kept saying that.

And then he felt quite unhappy because he began to think that he was going to die.

HECTOR CONTEMPLATES
HIS OWN DEATH

Hector had thought about death quite a lot during his life. He'd already seen quite a few people die in hospital when he was studying to be a doctor. He and his classmates were very young at the time, and most of the people who died in hospital were older, so they had the impression that death only happened to people of a different kind, even though they knew this wasn't true. But, as previously mentioned, knowing and feeling are two different things, and feeling is what counts.

He'd seen people die very peacefully, almost willingly. They were of several different sorts: those who were already frail from their illness, who felt that life had become too much of an effort and were quite relieved that it would soon be over; those who believed in the Good Lord, for whom death was just a journey, and it didn't make them sad at all; and then there were those who felt that they'd had a good life and couldn't complain if it ended now.

Of course it was mostly old people who were able to say that.

But, occasionally, somebody as young as Hector and his classmates would be admitted to the hospital suffering from a very, very serious illness, and each day they would watch this person grow thinner, suffer, weep and finally die. And even if they tried to see this as an opportunity to learn more about medicine, it shook them all the same.

When Hector had chosen to study psychiatry, he'd told himself that one advantage of that worthy profession was that you rarely saw your patients die. Whereas in some fields it was really dreadful (we won't mention any names so that if you ever have to go to one of those departments you won't worry in advance). Hector even knew specialists in those fields who'd been to see him because they ended up finding it hard to bear seeing their patients die. Hector had to give them quite a lot of pills as well as psychotherapy.

And, of course, Hector had already lost people he loved, but there again they had been older, except for one very good friend, and he occasionally imagined what age she would be now, and the conversations they might have had.

All this might explain why, locked in his storeroom that smelt of dead rat, Hector wasn't very scared of dying. Because when you think about something a lot, you become less and less scared of it.

He also said to himself that even if he died now, he'd already lived a good life: he'd had a nice mother and father, many very good friends, he'd fallen deeply in love more than once, had chosen a profession he loved, had been on some wonderful trips, had often felt he was helping people, and had never suffered any terrible misfortune. His life was a lot better than the lives of most people on the planet.

Of course, he hadn't had time to make any little Hectors or Hectorines, but this was just as well because now they would be orphans.

Fear of death, then, was not the most difficult thing. No. What made Hector miserable was thinking about the people he loved, who loved him and whom he'd never see again, and how unhappy they'd be when they found out that he was dead.

He thought about Clara, and how very sad she would be when she heard the news, and memories came flooding back of her laughing, crying, talking to him, sleeping pressed up beside him.

He could feel how much he loved her and she loved him, and how much she would suffer.

He also thought of Ying Li, but not as intensely because he had fewer memories of her. Ying Li was like a future that would never exist, that had never had much chance of existing.

He thought of old friends like Édouard and Jean-Michel, especially Jean-Michel, who might feel guilty because Hector had come here to see him.

And then he thought of his parents, and that was terrible, too, because although it often happens, it isn't normal for parents to outlive their child.

He remembered Marie-Louise's mother, who had never really come back to life after her husband died, and he wondered whether this would happen to Clara or his parents.

And he took out his notebook in order to write them a note, which they might find on him. He began by writing to Clara, telling her how much he loved her, and that she shouldn't be sad for too long because he thought he'd had a good life and in large part this was thanks to her.

Then he wrote to his parents, telling them that of course it was sad, but that he wasn't all that scared, and because his parents believed strongly in the Good Lord he thought that this message would help them.

He slipped the scraps of paper under his shirt, telling himself that this way the criminals wouldn't see them, but that the people undressing him to do the autopsy would. (Hector had seen quite a few autopsies, and it makes you think about death when you see that inside we're just a pile of soft, rather fragile organs.) Of course, there was the possibility that the criminals would make him disappear completely and that his body would never be found, but he preferred not to think about that.

And then he sat waiting on a beer crate, with the light bulb on the ceiling and the smell of dead rat. He felt his fear of death coming back a bit and so, to distract himself, he listened to the others.

The others were still arguing about the same thing: the optimist said that Hector would bring them a lot of money, the pessimist thought that Hector was more likely to bring them a lot of trouble, and the realist, the boss, felt that it would be better just to get rid of Hector. But the pessimist pointed out that the driver and the bodyguard, whom the other two had let go, might report that Hector had been kidnapped, and as he was white, the small army of white men in shorts might try to find whoever was responsible. And there weren't that many people there who put up real roadblocks manned by fake policemen, so they might trace it back to them.

When Hector heard this, he told himself that he had a slight chance.

He took out his notebook and began chewing his pen and thinking very hard.

And then he wrote a note, which he slipped under the door.

He heard the others go quiet.

You must be wondering what Hector wrote in his little notebook.

A magic formula known only to psychiatrists, which they are only allowed to use when their lives are in danger?

HECTOR IS SMART

Hector had simply written, 'You have a real problem there. We should talk.'

And so the door opened and one of the boss's two friends told Hector to come out, in a not very friendly voice. He wasn't even holding a revolver. Hector told himself that at least they'd understood that he was no fool and wasn't going to play Jackie Chan and try to knock them out with kicks in all directions.

The boss was still sitting down, holding Hector's note, and he said, 'What do you want to talk about?'

And so Hector explained that he was a visitor to this country and that he didn't want any problems. If they let him go he wouldn't tell the police anything.

The boss laughed, saying that if that was all he had to say he might as well have stayed in the storeroom.

Hector said that he wouldn't tell the police anything, and to prove it he wouldn't tell Eduardo anything either.

At this, they all opened their eyes wide, a bit like the other two in the car earlier. Except for the boss, who asked him very calmly, 'You know Eduardo?'

Hector said that he knew Eduardo quite well, but above all he knew his wife, who was suffering from a deep depression. Because, well, he was a psychiatrist.

The others had gone quiet, and then one of the boss's

friends, who had kept Hector's wallet, looked inside it and almost screamed, 'It's true, he's a *spychiatrist!*'

'Shut up, you moron!' said the boss.

Hector could see that the boss was thinking very hard. If Hector was telling the truth, he wouldn't say anything to the police, because if he knew Eduardo and his wife he couldn't be that interested in helping the police. But if Hector really was Eduardo's friend and he told him what had happened, Eduardo might not like it and life could become a little difficult for the boss. In that case, the sooner Hector disappeared the better. Then again, if the police and the small army of white men began searching for the boss and his gang, life wouldn't be easy either, especially if Eduardo got mixed up in it as well. On the other hand, if the boss let Hector go and he reported them to the police, it would also be a problem, except that since Hector would still be alive, the police wouldn't think it worth wasting their energy on – rather like in Hector's country when you go and complain that somebody has stolen your car radio.

Hector was counting on the fact that bosses are usually smart, and that the boss of this gang was going to think about all this and make the right decision: to free Hector.

The boss looked at Hector and he saw the notebook sticking out of his pocket. He made one of his men bring it over and opened it at the first page:

Lesson no. 1: Making comparisons can spoil your happiness.

Lesson no. 2: Happiness often comes when least expected.

Lesson no. 3: Many people see happiness only in their future.

Lesson no. 4: Many people think that happiness comes from having more power or more money.

Lesson no. 5: Sometimes happiness is not knowing the whole story.

Ying Li Ying Li YING LI Hector Ying Li Hector YING LI Hector Ying Li Clara.

Lesson no. 6: Happiness is a long walk in beautiful, unfamiliar mountains.

Lesson no. 7: It's a mistake to think that happiness is the goal.

Lesson no. 8: Happiness is being with the people you love.

Lesson no. 8b: Unhappiness is being separated from the people you love.

Lesson no. 9: Happiness is knowing your family lacks for nothing.

Lesson no. 10: Happiness is doing a job you love.

Lesson no. 11: Happiness is having a home and a garden of your own.

Lesson no. 12: It's harder to be happy in a country run by bad people.

Lesson no. 13: Happiness is feeling useful to others.

Lesson no. 14: Happiness is to be loved for exactly who you are.

Observation: People are kinder to a child who smiles (very important).

The boss read through to the end then he looked at Hector and said, 'All right, let him go.'

HECTOR CELEBRATES

Hector was on yet another plane, and you'll never guess what, he was sitting in the most expensive part of the plane, the part with seats that stretch right out and a private TV screen and air hostesses who smile and bring you lots of champagne.

This time he'd paid for it himself, even though he couldn't really afford it. He knew that when he got back he'd have lots of calls from the lady who looked after his bank account, but he'd decided that he was going to do whatever he liked for a while, because he'd realised that life could end very suddenly. (Of course he'd known this for a long time, but, as we keep telling you, knowing and feeling are not the same things.)

Since his spell in the storeroom that smelt of dead rat, Hector felt that life was wonderful.

He knew that this feeling wouldn't last, because he'd treated people who'd had near-death experiences – during the war, for example, in the camps where almost everybody had died, and even a man whose boat had sunk and who'd spent a long time in the water waiting to be rescued.

These people had told him that, just after being saved, they too had felt life was wonderful. But they had soon become caught up in life's everyday problems, big or small (not counting the people who'd been haunted for years by terrible memories). And now these people who had been close to death fretted over their tax returns or because the neighbours had the TV on too loud, just like everybody else.

And so Hector wanted to make the most of this feeling while it lasted.

The night he'd nearly died, everybody had fêted him when he got back to Marie-Louise's house, everybody was laughing and crying at the same time, and Jean-Michel and Marcel were there.

Marie-Louise's family hadn't called the police because they had expected that the criminals would demand a ransom for Hector's release. Calling the police might have complicated matters, and anyway, some of the policemen might have wanted some of the ransom money, because in this country they weren't very well paid. As the criminals had let Hector come back with the car (just so as not to upset Eduardo in case he heard about it), there hadn't even been a theft. It was as though the whole thing had never happened, and there was no need to tell the police or the army of men in shorts or anybody else.

A big party started up in the middle of the night.

Even so, Hector went to see the chauffeur and the bodyguard, who were waiting shamefaced in the kitchen, because Marie-Louise and Nestor had given them a severe ticking off. They tried to explain that none of it was their fault, the criminals had driven off so fast (and no doubt they had been so scared) that they hadn't had time to tell them that Hector was still in the car. Hector told them not to worry about it, and that he'd tell Marie-Louise and Nestor not to tick them off again.

Hector was so happy to feel alive that he wanted everybody to be happy. And that was good, because they were.

It was very late, but nobody felt like going to bed, and even people in the neighbouring houses had woken up and come to the party. There was music and everyone danced – everybody danced very, very well, even the older men and women who were the same age as Hector's parents. Even Hector, who didn't know how to dance very well, danced. But when you're very happy you don't mind about feeling clumsy, and when you're the hero of the evening your dance partners forgive you, especially Marie-Louise's pretty cousin with whom he didn't dance too badly and who continued to smile at him like she had earlier, during dinner. And there was also a lot to drink, all kinds of rum cocktails and some of that excellent beer – the same one that was in the crate Hector had sat on in the storeroom as he waited to die.

But Hector was no longer thinking about death, especially not when Marie-Louise's cousin took him upstairs. They went into a bedroom that couldn't have been used for some time. There was some old furniture and some family photos from the time when things weren't so bad in that country, and Hector had the impression of going into his grandparents' bedroom when he was a little boy. But the impression didn't last long because the cousin led him over to the bed (or did Hector lead her? It's difficult to know) and they did the things people do when they're in love, with the music drifting up through the floorboards.

Afterwards, Hector felt a little tired, but Marie-Louise's cousin didn't at all, and they went back down to join the people who were still dancing. Hector felt a bit embarrassed, but very quickly he realised that either people hadn't noticed or they thought it was very good that he'd gone upstairs with Marie-Louise's cousin.

Later on, he came upon Nestor, who was opening a beer, and Nestor winked at him. As the music was blaring, he drew near and spoke rather loudly into Hector's ear.

'So, how is your investigation into happiness going?'

'Not bad, not bad,' Hector replied, rather awkwardly.

Nestor laughed, and spoke into Hector's ear again.

'Here, there are plenty of reasons to be unhappy, even for people like us who are relatively fortunate. So when there's an occasion to be happy we want to make the most of it! We don't care about the next day, we never know what it might bring!'

Just then, the pretty cousin, who'd begun to dance with Jean-Michel (because although Jean-Michel wasn't really interested in girls, he'd always danced like a god), gave Hector a big smile and that Hector understood very well, even better than Nestor's explanations.

In the plane, Hector took out his little notebook again.

Lesson no. 15: Happiness comes when you feel truly alive.

This wasn't bad, but it didn't explain it very well. He chewed his pencil and then wrote:

Lesson no. 16: Happiness is knowing how to celebrate.

He remembered Édouard, who was fond of celebrating –

like on that first evening in China. And there's no point in telling you what Hector thought about next, because even if you're not a psychiatrist you've no doubt guessed.

HECTOR GAINS PERSPECTIVE

HECTOR continued to drink the champagne brought to him by the nice air hostesses, and he felt very content. But this didn't stop him from thinking about happiness, because he was serious about his investigation.

Firstly, why did drinking champagne (or very good beer, or the excellent wines Édouard liked) make almost everybody happy? All over the world, people drank these grown-up drinks in order to celebrate, and it always worked, it always made people happier and everybody felt jolly at the same time.

Unfortunately, some people when they drank too much did very stupid things, like driving very badly and causing accidents, picking fights, and doing what people in love do, but with anybody and everybody so they caught nasty diseases. Other people drank so often that it no longer had much effect on them. And so they never stopped drinking and became more and more ill. (Édouard, over there in China, was perhaps not far from that slippery slope.)

That made Hector think: if drinking made people happier and at the same time affected their brain (you only need to hear somebody speaking who has drunk too much), that meant there was an area of the brain that made you happy and that became more active when you drank. Hector felt pleased, this would be a good question to ask the professor of Happiness Studies.

And what about the pills the pharmaceutical companies made? For the time being, they were only able to lift people's mood to where it had been before they started feeling very sad or very scared. But what if one day a pharmaceutical company invented a pill that made you happier than you'd ever been before? Would he want to prescribe it to his patients? He wasn't sure.

He took out his little notebook and wrote:

Question: Is happiness simply a chemical reaction in the brain?

To reward himself for having thought hard, Hector gestured to the air hostess, who came over, smiling, to fill his glass. He thought she was very pretty, but he knew that this might also be the effect of the champagne, and anyway life was complicated enough already with Clara, Ying Li and Marie-Louise's cousin, who had told him that she occasionally went on holiday to his country.

He wondered why he wasn't as in love with her as he was with Ying Li, but if you've been concentrating you'll already have guessed: Hector had only shared enjoyment with Marie-Louise's cousin (we won't say her name in case you bump into her in Hector's city). With Ying Li he'd shared everything, enjoyment and sorrow. With Clara, too, of course, but for some time now they'd shared too much frustration, boredom and fatigue.

He would have liked to discuss all this with somebody, but there was nobody next to him because he was in a part of the plane that was so expensive it was almost empty. Even if there had been somebody, he would have had to lean over a long way because the armrests were so wide. This was interesting because it meant that for rich people happiness was being able to feel on their own, at any rate when they were on a plane.

Whereas for poor people, like the women on their oilcloths, happiness was being surrounded by their friends. But it's true that you never know on a plane whether the person next to you will be a friend, so it's best to take precautions.

Just then, an air hostess came up from the lower deck where the seats were less expensive, and went to talk to her fellow air hostesses. They looked quite worried. Hector wondered whether it was because there was a problem with the plane, and he got ready to think about death again, though much more comfortably here than in the storeroom.

One of the hostesses came over and asked if there was a doctor among the passengers. Hector felt uncomfortable: as a psychiatrist you are a real doctor, but because of listening to people's problems all the time, you often get out of the habit of treating ordinary illnesses. Also, he wondered whether the air hostess was asking for a doctor because there was a lady on the plane having a baby. He'd always been nervous about this when travelling by train or plane. When he was a student, he'd never gone into the wards where women had babies. Of course he'd studied the subject, but only very briefly the night before the exam, and he'd forgotten most of it, and in any case studying and reality are not the same things. And so he felt rather uncomfortable, but even so he signalled to the air hostess and he told her that he was a real doctor.

The air hostess was very glad, because she'd looked in the other sections of the plane and there were no doctors, or at any rate nobody who wanted to say that they were. (Hector understood why later, as will you.)

And so, Hector left his little paradise and followed the air hostess down into economy class. Everybody in the rows of seats looked up at him as he went by because they'd understood that he was a doctor, and this worried him slightly; what would he do if they all took it into their heads to demand a consultation?

The air hostess took him over to a lady who didn't look very well.

Hector began speaking to her, but it was difficult because she had a very bad headache, and she didn't speak Hector's language. When she spoke in English, she had an accent which Hector and the air hostess found quite difficult to understand.

Her face was slightly swollen, like people who drink too much, but she didn't look as if she'd been drinking. Finally, she took a piece of paper out of her bag and handed it to Hector. It was a medical report: this was much easier to understand for a doctor. Six months ago, the lady had had an operation inside her head because a small piece of her brain had begun to grow in a way it shouldn't, and this bad growth had been removed. Then Hector noticed that her hair wasn't her own, it was a wig. Since hair grows back in six months, Hector understood that the lady had been given medication that had made her face swell up and her hair fall out, and that the growth must have been very bad indeed. The lady studied him while he was reading the report of the surgery, as if she were trying to tell from his face what he made of it all. But Hector had been trained to have a reassuring look at all times and he said to her, 'Don't worry. I'm just going to ask you some questions.'

And he spoke to her like a doctor, in order to find out how long she'd had the headache, and whether it was a throbbing pain like a heart beat, or more like toothache, and which part of her head hurt most. He examined her eyes with a small torch the air hostess lent him. He asked the lady to squeeze his hands in hers, and other things you learn in order to become a doctor. And the lady seemed less anxious than when he'd arrived.

Asking those questions and doing those tests had taken Hector's mind off the thought that this lady might die, but once he'd finished he was forced to think about it again.

Just then, the air hostess handed him the lady's passport, and he saw in the photograph, which was less than a year old, a beautiful young woman who had the same eyes as the woman now looking at him, and he understood that the illness had also stolen her beauty.

He remembered lesson no. 14: *Happiness is to be loved for exactly who you are.*

And so he smiled at her, because men's smiles must be something she greatly missed.

HECTOR DOES A BIT OF HISTORY
AND GEOGRAPHY

HER name was Djamila, which happens to mean beautiful, and she came from an equally beautiful country, where people a little older than Hector would have gone on holiday when they were young, because you could smoke weed in the midst of magnificent mountains. The girls would have brought back beautiful fabrics, which they turned into dresses and curtains. (It was a time when dresses and curtains looked very similar.)

Since then, that country had always been at war, at first because it had been invaded by a large neighbouring country that had wanted to create a heaven on earth, except that the inhabitants of the beautiful country didn't agree with their version of heaven. So the inhabitants had fought for years against the soldiers from the large neighbouring country and the war had become like a festering sore that made the big country very sick. After that, things went from bad to worse for everybody, countless mothers had shed countless tears, the big country had grown as weak as a small country, and Djamila's country had gone on being at war because some people there also wanted to create heaven on earth. (Be very wary of people who declare that they're going to create heaven on earth, they almost invariably create hell.) The beautiful country had grown poorer than when Hector was a child. It was getting better now;

a large army made up of people from countries all over the world had gone to sort things out (but they didn't wear shorts because it was too cold) and people had renewed hope.

Except Djamila, who can't have had much hope, and who was trying to find reasons to have some by studying Hector's face as he read her medical report written by another doctor, a medical report that, as you've guessed, wasn't very hopeful.

Hector told her that he would look after her until the end of the flight.

He put on his doctorly air and told the air hostess that Djamila needed to be able to stretch out, that it would relieve her headache, and that they must take her to the seat next to his so that he could keep an eye on her. The air hostess called over a very kind steward. The three of them helped Djamila to get up and walk to the other section of the plane. When she stood up Djamila was tall, but she weighed very little.

When she was sitting next to Hector in a very comfortable seat that stretched out almost like a bed, she smiled for the first time, and Hector recognised the Djamila from the passport photograph. He asked her whether she still had a headache, and she said she had, but that being there made her feel better, and that Hector was too kind.

They continued talking. Hector thought that it might help her to forget about her headache, and as he spoke to her he looked at her pupils, the way doctors do.

They were both going to the big country where there were more psychiatrists than anywhere else in the world. Notice that we say 'more psychiatrists than anywhere else in the world' but we could just as well say more swimming pools, more Nobel prizewinners, more strategic bombers, more apple pies, more computers, more natural parks, more libraries, more cheer-leaders, more serial killers, more newspapers, more racoons, more of many more things, because it was the country of More, and had been for a long time. No doubt because the people who lived there had left their own countries precisely because they wanted more, especially more freedom. (The only people who hadn't got more freedom were the natives who already lived there, but, as previously mentioned, that was in the days when people who came from countries like Hector's tended to think that everything belonged to them.)

Djamila was going to visit her sister who had married a citizen of that country. She was going to stay with them for a while.

Hector explained that he was going there to meet a professor who was a specialist in Happiness Studies. He immediately regretted saying this, because he told himself that happiness probably wasn't a very good subject to discuss with Djamila.

But she smiled at him, and explained that, for her, happiness was knowing that her country was going to be a better place, that her little brothers weren't going to grow up to be killed in the war, and that her sister had a kind husband and children who could go to school, go on holiday and grow up to be doctors or lawyers or forest rangers or painters or whatever they wished.

Hector noticed that she didn't speak of her own happiness, but that of others, of the people she loved.

And then Djamila said that her head had started hurting a bit more. Hector called the air hostess and told her that he wanted to speak to the captain. (You can do that if you're a doctor.) After a while, the captain arrived in his fine uniform with his equally fine moustache. (Don't worry, another pilot was in the cockpit flying the plane.) Hector explained the situation to him and the captain asked if it would help if he made the plane fly a little lower.

Hector said that they could always try. This is something that both pilots and doctors know: if something is causing pressure in your body, being high up, like at the top of a mountain or in an aeroplane, increases the pressure because the air around you has less pressure, even though the plane is pressurised. And so the captain rushed off to make the plane descend.

Djamila told Hector that she felt he was going to too much trouble, really, and he said that he wasn't and that he liked talking to the captain and making the plane descend, and that next time he might even ask him to do a loop the loop to make Djamila's headache better. This made her laugh and again he saw the Djamila in the passport photograph.

Then he asked the air hostess for some champagne, because it couldn't do Djamila any harm.

They clinked glasses, and Djamila told him that this was the first time she'd drunk champagne, because in her country it had been banned for a long time, and all you could find was cheap vodka left behind by the defeated soldiers. She tasted the champagne, and said it was wonderful, and Hector said he couldn't have agreed more.

Hector recalled the last lesson, *Happiness is knowing how to celebrate,* and he wanted Djamila to benefit from it.

After they had talked a little longer, her headache was better, and then she fell peacefully asleep.

The passengers around them were concerned. They could see through the windows that the plane was flying lower. And so the air hostesses explained why, and the passengers looked at Hector and Djamila and felt reassured.

Hector was thinking as he sat next to Djamila who was asleep.

Djamila must think about death often. He had thought about it for less than an hour in his storeroom. But for her, it was as if she'd been living in that storeroom for months. And yet she continued to smile.

And she had told him that she was pleased that her country and her family had a better chance of being happy.

He picked up his little notebook and wrote:

Lesson no. 17: Happiness is caring about the happiness of those you love.

HECTOR HAS A DREAM

THE pilot with the fine moustache landed the plane very well, without a bump, and everybody clapped, perhaps because they'd felt a little worried when the plane wasn't flying very high. And so a smooth landing made them happy, when normally it didn't have much effect on them.

Another case of comparison, Hector told himself.

As the passengers left the aeroplane, throwing them quick glances, he waited with Djamila and the air hostess until the doctors whom the pilot had asked for over the radio arrived. Djamila had woken up, and fortunately her pupils were still the same and she was able to squeeze Hector's hands equally hard with both her hands, though not very hard of course because she was a girl, and because she wasn't very well.

Two big strapping men in white coats arrived with a wheelchair to take Djamila away, and Hector wanted to explain to them what was wrong with her. But they didn't listen to him. First they asked Djamila whether she had any insurance. Before treating Djamila they wanted to know whether she could pay! And they weren't even doctors, because in that country doctors don't usually go out on call, they wait for patients to be brought to them. Hector became a little angry, but Djamila told him that it wasn't worth it, that her sister had taken out all the necessary insurance, that in any case she'd be waiting for her here at the airport, and that her sister's husband's father was a doctor. She would be well taken care of and Hector could go.

And so they exchanged telephone numbers in order to keep in touch and Hector left. He looked back one last time at Djamila sitting very upright in her wheelchair between the two nurses; she smiled and gave him a last little wave goodbye.

Hector had arrived in a huge city by the sea, in a place where the weather was always good and there were even palm trees growing in the gardens. The city was as big as some countries. It was criss-crossed by motorways, which you could see from the sky. Gazing out of the window in the plane, Hector had thought that it looked as if somebody had tossed spaghetti onto the very elaborate carpet that was the city, with its glittering blue gemstones: the swimming pools. For there were a great many swimming pools.

Hector described his trip to Agnès, who had come to pick him up at the airport, and was now driving a big car along one of the motorways he'd seen from the plane. The sky was blue and the air shimmered with heat, but not in the car because Agnès had put the air conditioning on full. Hector remembered that unlike many girls she didn't feel the cold at all.

Agnès had been Hector's girlfriend, but one day they had separated. Actually, Hector had left Agnès, because he was very young at the time and didn't know enough to recognise a really nice girl when he saw one, because he hadn't met any others. And so he had left Agnès to go and meet other girls who were not nearly as well suited to him, but he didn't know that then and only realised it much later. But by then Agnès had already left for the big country of More, and she'd married a boy from there and even had three children by him. But Agnès and Hector had stayed friends, because they liked each other, even without doing the things people do when they're in love.

When Hector told her about Djamila, Agnès was alarmed.

'You don't realise what an incredible risk you took! People here sue doctors all the time and their lawyers claim huge amounts of compensation. And on that plane it's the same as if you'd been here. What's more, your insurance wouldn't have covered you. It's lucky that everything went well!'

Hector explained that in any event Djamila was a nice person, and not the type who would sue a doctor, but at the same time now he understood why he'd been the only doctor the air hostesses could find on the plane; the others must have been worried about prospective meetings with lawyers. They'd looked away, like when you don't want to be asked to go to the blackboard.

Hector knew a few lawyers, and they didn't scare him; he just found them a little tiresome when they talked too much at dinner parties. But Agnès explained that, over here, they were truly fearsome and that they earned as much money as Édouard. (Agnès also knew Édouard, who'd been a little bit in love with her when they were very young, but Agnès had been in love with Hector at the time – love is complicated.)

Agnès lived in a very nice house with a big lawn, palm trees, and a kidney-shaped swimming pool. Agnès's husband wasn't bad either; for Hector it was a bit like having a brother who always came first in games. His name was Alan and he was very kind to Hector, except that every evening he asked him if he'd like to go jogging with him the next morning, because Alan began every day with a three-mile run. Since he did this at six thirty in the morning, Hector didn't really want to go running; he preferred to stay in bed dreaming, because dreams are very important to psychiatrists.

While Alan went running and Agnès made breakfast for the children before taking them to school, Hector dreamt about Ying Li, although sometimes he muddled everything up: instead of Djamila having a headache on the plane it was Ying Li and he tried to save her by squeezing her hands very hard. Later, it was Hector who was sitting in the wheelchair, and Clara was pushing him down the aisle between the seats. And the pilot who came to see him was the old Chinese monk, who was still dressed like a monk but with a pilot's cap, and who kept looking at him and laughing, because Hector was back in his seat on the plane again, but he was stark naked, and he didn't dare get up out of his seat for fear the other passengers and the air hostesses would notice. The person sitting next to him put a hand on his arm to comfort him, and it was Ying Li, but also Clara and Marie-Louise's cousin and Djamila, all of them one woman who loved him and was smiling at him, and this was happiness, but then he woke up.

He reached for his notebook and wrote:

Lesson no. 18: Happiness could be the freedom to love more than one woman at the same time.

The problem, of course, was that women wouldn't agree.

He crossed out the sentence and then did lots of little squiggles on it, because he was a bit afraid that Clara might one day find his notebook and read it.

HECTOR GOES TO THE BEACH
AND DOES SOME MATHS

ALAN and Agnès's house was in one of the most attractive parts of this city that was as big as a small country, right near the sea. And so one morning Hector walked down the street lined with trees and pretty wooden houses, some of them quite old (in this city old meant the same age as an old person). Then he went down some steps cut into the cliff, walked below the roaring traffic, and came out onto a huge white sandy beach, which he crossed to go and wade in the sea, which was quite cold. When his feet were in the water, he looked at the vast blue horizon and told himself that this sea stretched all the way to China. This little wave lapping at his ankles might have come from the very city where he'd met Ying Li.

The funny thing was that there weren't many people on this magnificent beach, and hardly anybody like Hector, Agnès or Alan. There were mostly poor people with rather a lot of children, or black people who were generally quite young. Hector understood that in this country rich people were either too busy to go to the beach because they worked a lot, like Alan and Agnès, or they preferred the nice clean water in their swimming pools or Jacuzzis, or they weren't too keen on mixing with poor people, but this of course was true in all countries.

In fact, there were other beaches further north of the city, where rich people and even film stars lived. But in places like that you didn't have the right to go on the beach unless you lived there, because in this country you could even buy a beach if you had enough money.

So, the poor people had this huge beach all to themselves, free of charge, and they had fun playing volleyball, drinking beer, picking up girls, and they seemed quite happy, because here on the beach they could forget about the people who were richer than them, who had nice cars, nice houses and expensive lawyers.

Hector put on his sunglasses and wrote:

Lesson no. 19: The sun and the sea make everybody happy.

And he told himself that if one day he became really poor, he would seek refuge in a sunny city by the sea and in a poor country so that he would feel less poor. (Remember lesson no. 1: *Making comparisons can spoil your happiness.*)

He looked at his list of lessons and felt that he was gradually coming to the end. More and more now, when something that happened on his trip made him think about happiness, he realised that it corresponded to one of the lessons he'd already written down. This meant that either he'd learnt almost all there was to learn or that he was going round in circles and it was time to show his list to somebody else. (For the moment, the only person who'd read the whole thing was the boss of the gang, but he hadn't told Hector what he thought.)

That evening, Hector had dinner with Alan, Agnès and the

children. He was glad to be in a proper family with a father, a mother, two little boys and a little girl, because it seemed to him like a good place to find happiness. The problem was that the children didn't stay at the table very long; they went out to play in the garden, came back to have cake or went up to their rooms to watch TV or play computer games.

This annoyed Agnès, who wanted them to stay longer at the table, but Alan didn't seem too concerned, and he talked to Hector about his job. Alan wasn't only good at games, he was equally good at maths, and he calculated very complicated things. In fact he calculated calculations of calculations, and then other people who weren't as good at maths used his calculations to make their computers work or decipher the genetic code. (We won't go into what that is here, it would take too long, you'd be better looking it up in a dictionary.) Since Alan liked maths a lot, in his spare time he made up maths puzzles for an important newspaper, the type you can never work out and which make you feel like a complete moron.

'You should tell the children to stay at the table!' said Agnès.

'They don't want to,' Alan replied.

'Of course they won't want to it if they know that's okay with you.'

'It's not particularly okay with me, but I don't want to fight with the children while I'm having my dinner.'

' "My dinner", exactly! Well, I'd like it to be "our dinner", a family dinner.'

'They're kids. They get bored at the table. I was the same.'

'That's not what your mother says. She had proper dinners, sitting with her children.'

'Yes, well, I don't have very happy memories of them. Listening to my mother moaning every evening.'

Then Agnès looked upset.

'Are you saying that that's what I'm doing? Boring you with my moaning?'

'No, but it's true that we keep having this same conversation.'

'Is it? Well, we wouldn't have to have it at all if you had a little more authority over the children!'

'They're not misbehaving, they're just enjoying themselves.'

'They're watching stupid TV series! Instead of talking with their parents.'

'There are other times besides dinner.'

'When? You work all day. I'm the one who spends the most time with them.'

'Well, that means they converse with their mother.'

'Parents means both a father and a mother in case you hadn't noticed.'

'Not always. My father cleared off when I was still quite young.'

'And look at the result: you weren't set an example of how to look after your children!'

'No, but I had the example of a guy who ended up clearing off because his wife never stopped complaining!'

Hector felt very uncomfortable; it reminded him of when he was in his consulting room and a man and a woman argued in front of him, except that this was different because they were his friends, and it was happening in their nice kitchen.

Alan and Agnès suddenly realised that Hector was feeling

uncomfortable, and they said, 'Sorry,' and everybody tried to have a normal conversation. Hector explained the aim of his trip and the lessons he'd already learnt.

This made Alan think: he pointed out that maybe it was possible to calculate happiness.

'Calculate happiness?' Agnès and Hector asked.

'Yes. If happiness depends on various factors – for example, health, friends, having a job you like – we could gather all these elements together into a formula. Each factor would have a different coefficient and in the end we'd have a result, a happiness ratio . . . Or a happiness quotient, yes, an HQ!'

Hector took out his notebook and showed it to Alan and Agnès. (He was very glad that he'd crossed out lesson no. 18, because Agnès certainly wouldn't have liked it much either.) Together they tried to think up corresponding words for each of the lessons.

In some cases this was simple. For example, lesson no. 8: *Happiness is being with the people you love* could be 'love/ friendship' and 8b would be 'loneliness/isolation' – giving it a negative coefficient (don't worry if you don't know what that means, Alan knows). For lesson no. 4: *Many people think that happiness comes from having more power or more money* you could put 'social status' or 'money'.

But you try finding words for lessons like no. 5: *Sometimes happiness is not knowing the whole story* or no. 7: *It's a mistake to think that happiness is the goal,* and you'll see that it's like Alan's puzzles in the newspaper: you can't come up with the right answer.

Eventually they produced a list:

Being loved Money Feeling useful

Friendship Health Social status Work you enjoy

Celebration Happiness of those you love Peace of mind

In the end, they couldn't think of any other words. And then Alan looked at Agnès and said, 'Being married.' And for a moment Agnès had tears in her eyes.

HECTOR LEARNS ABOUT
FAMILY LIFE

THE next day, Hector woke up quite early so that Agnès could take him in to work with her. This time they didn't go on the motorway because there was rather a lot of traffic at that time of day. So Hector was able to get a better idea of what the city looked like, and it didn't look like anything he'd ever seen. There were avenues of beautiful houses, some whitewashed in the Spanish style, some made of red brick with small windows in the English style, some made of teak beach-house style, some Austrian chalet style, or modern and made entirely of glass, and there were many more styles besides, as if the architects had been having fun by trying out all the different themes. And Hector saw other areas, with supermarkets, garages, parking lots, and petrol stations, like in a big suburb. And neighbourhoods full of modern buildings and people wearing suits despite the sky that was always blue and the heat. And areas in the middle of the city with oil wells and vacant lots where young black boys played basketball.

In the car, of course, Hector asked Agnès if she was happy.

'I knew you'd ask me that and so I thought about it last night. I think I'm happy. I have a job I love, a husband I love, and children who are happy. In fact, all I want is for things to stay as they are. The only shadow on my happiness is when I tell myself sometimes that as it's all going well, it can't last, that one day things won't be so good.'

'You say: "I think I'm happy." What allows you to say that? Is it comparing yourself to others?'

'Not entirely. You can't really know how other people experience happiness or misfortune. In fact, I'm comparing myself to myself! I think of other times in my life, and it feels like I've never been so happy.'

Hector found the idea of comparing yourself to yourself interesting. Comparisons can spoil your happiness (lesson no. 1), but they can also help you to tell yourself that you're happy. Hector also thought that this meant Agnès was happier now than when she'd been with him. On the one hand he understood quite well why, but on the other it still upset him a bit, because that's what men are like.

Since he carried on thinking without speaking, Agnès went on, 'Of course, things aren't always rosy. You saw us arguing about the children. But that's normal for a couple who have children, I suppose.'

Speaking of children, Hector asked her whether having them made people happier. Agnès said that it brought moments of great joy, but also quite a few worries; you had to think about them all the time, and you could kiss goodbye to having a lie-in for years to come, and this idea alone terrified Hector.

She also worried about her children's future in this country where children were going a bit crazy. Hector said that children in his country were also going a bit crazy, but of course, as Agnès lived in the country of More, the crazy children there were going that little bit more crazy, and so instead of every day hitting other schoolmates who weren't as strong, or girls, or even their teachers, like in Hector's country, they went straight ahead and shot them with weapons made for grown-ups.

'That's why I was complaining last night. I don't want my children to be brought up by television and video games. But that's what's happening to children in rich countries and in poor countries, too. We're very concerned about polluting the air, but not about polluting our children's minds.'

And Agnès went on talking, because it was a subject that was very important to her. She was even doing a study on it. She would show small children a film of a man hitting a doll then leave them to play together and compare the number of times they hit each other (not very hard thankfully because they were only little). And, well, they hit each other noticeably more after they'd seen the film than before. Because, Agnès explained, children learn a lot through imitation, they're made that way, and that's why if your mummy and daddy are kind you'll be kind.

You must be thinking that Agnès was a psychiatrist, but she wasn't, she was a psychologist. A psychologist is somebody who studies how people think or why they go a bit crazy or what makes children learn at school and why some don't, or why they hit their schoolmates. Psychologists, unlike psychiatrists, don't have the right to prescribe pills, but they can make people take tests or choose the right picture in a box or calculate things using dominoes, or tell them what an ink stain makes them think of. And after that they know something about the way your mind works (but they don't understand everything, it has to be said).

Hector asked Agnès if she felt happy when she was working on this study of children. Agnès said that she did, because she felt useful to others (lesson no. 13, thought Hector).

They arrived at the university where Agnès worked, and Alan too incidentally, because that's where they'd met. What was funny was that you'd think the university dated back to the Middle Ages or just after: it had splendid old buildings with little bell towers, and pillars, and statues and rolling lawns. In fact, the university was no older than an old person, but people here had wanted their university to be as splendid as the ones in Hector's country. And so they'd built a copy and invented a style called 'New Medieval'. It really was the country of More.

There were a lot of students of all colours walking across the lawns, and some pretty Chinese girls in shorts who made Hector think of you-know-who, but he tried to concentrate; he had come here to work hard.

Because it was here that the important professor who was a world expert on happiness worked. He had been studying happiness for years, he gave talks on it at conferences and had become very well known – not as well known as a TV presenter, but quite well known all the same, especially among other happiness experts. Agnès knew him well; he'd been her professor. And so she had mentioned Hector to him and the important professor had agreed to talk to him, and then Hector would be able to show him his list.

Hector felt rather nervous, like before you go up to the blackboard, because although when he'd written them he'd thought his little lessons were very interesting, and even when he'd reread them the night before with Agnès and Alan, now that he was about to show them to the professor he thought they were rather silly.

He told Agnès this, but she said that he was mistaken, that the lessons were a measure of his experience, and that Hector's way of seeing things was no less valid than the results of any laboratory experiments.

And Hector told himself that she really was a very nice girl, and that when you're young you can sometimes be very foolish.

HECTOR LEARNS THAT HE IS
NOT TOTALLY STUPID

THE important professor was tiny, but he had a very long nose and a tuft of hair sticking up from his head, like the plumage of a bird. He spoke in a very loud voice and looked at Hector from time to time and said 'huh?' as if he expected Hector to say 'yes, of course'. But he didn't give him time to say that before continuing his story.

'Happiness. We're tearing our hair out to try to find a definition of it, for heaven's sake. Is it joy? People will tell you that it isn't, that joy is a fleeting emotion, a moment of happiness, which is always welcome, mind you. And then what about pleasure, huh? Oh, yes, that's easy, everybody knows what that is, but there again it doesn't last. But is happiness not the sum total of lots of small joys and pleasures, huh? Well, my colleagues have finally agreed on the term "Subjective well-being". Ugh, how dry and lifeless, it sounds like the sort of term a lawyer would use: "My client wishes to press charges for an infringement of his subjective well-being!" I mean to say, whatever next, huh?'

Hector found him quite extraordinary as he paced up and down talking, as if he wanted to take up as much space as possible. He also sensed that he was very learned.

Finally, Hector showed him his list.

'Oh yes,' said the professor, putting on a small pair of

spectacles, 'Agnès was telling me about it. She's a splendid girl, huh? I've known many students, but she really is very intelligent, and charming, too . . .'

While he was reading the list, Hector wondered whether the professor was going to think that he was not only not very intelligent but very naïve, or even very stupid. And so he felt nervous, but at the same time he told himself that when you've escaped death you shouldn't be nervous of a professor who says 'huh?'

The professor was reading his list. Hector had copied it out onto a clean sheet of paper, and this is what it looked like – in case you've forgotten:

Lesson no. 1: Making comparisons can spoil your happiness.

Lesson no. 2: Happiness often comes when least expected.

Lesson no. 3: Many people see happiness only in their future.

Lesson no. 4: Many people think that happiness comes from having more power or more money.

Lesson no. 5: Sometimes happiness is not knowing the whole story.

Lesson no. 6: Happiness is a long walk in beautiful, unfamilar mountains.

Lesson no. 7: It's a mistake to think that happiness is the goal.

Lesson no. 8: Happiness is being with the people you love.

Lesson no. 8b: Unhappiness is being separated from the people you love.

Lesson no. 9: Happiness is knowing your family lacks for nothing.

Lesson no. 10: Happiness is doing a job you love.

Lesson no. 11: Happiness is having a home and a garden of your own.

Lesson no. 12: It's harder to be happy in a country run by bad people.

Lesson no. 13: Happiness is feeling useful to others.

Lesson no. 14: Happiness is to be loved for exactly who you are.

Observation: People are kinder to a child who smiles (very important).

Lesson no. 15: Happiness comes when you feel truly alive.

Lesson no. 16: Happiness is knowing how to celebrate.

Lesson no. 17: Happiness is caring about the happiness of those you love.

Lesson no. 19: The sun and the sea make everybody happy.

The professor chuckled to himself as he read the list, and Hector felt uneasy, but he tried to find a comforting thought, and finally he came up with one: 'Happiness is not attaching too much importance to what other people think.' That might make a good lesson no. 18 to replace the one he'd crossed out.

Finally, the professor looked at the list and then looked at Hector.

'How funny, you've managed to include nearly all of them!'

'Nearly all of what?'

'The determinants of happiness. Well, the ones that we're researching. It's not totally stupid, this list of yours.'

'Do you mean to say that all these lessons could be valid?'

'Yes, pretty much. For each lesson I can find twenty or so studies that show, for example' – he looked at the list – 'that our happiness depends on comparisons, like in your lesson no. 1. Look, I'm going to ask you three questions. First I'll ask you to think about the difference between the life you have and the life you wish you had.'

Hector thought about it, and then he said that he was quite happy with his life and that above all he'd like it to continue as it was.

Of course, he would have liked to meet Ying Li again and to love Clara at the same time, but all he said to the professor was, 'I wouldn't mind having a more stable love life.'

The professor sighed as if to say: 'Ah! Wouldn't we all . . .' And then he asked Hector to think about another difference: between his life as it was now and the best period of his life in the past.

Hector said that he had happy childhood memories, but that he felt that his life now was more interesting. He remembered that Agnès also thought that she was happier now than in the past. For Charles on the plane, it had been a little bit the other way round. He remembered having flown first class and thought he was worse off in business class.

'Third question, third difference,' said the professor. 'Think about the difference between what you have and what others have.'

Hector found this question very interesting. In his country poor people were richer than most other people in the world, but knowing this didn't make them any happier, because every day they saw their richer fellow countrymen enjoying lots of nice things that they as poor people couldn't afford. And TV adverts reminded them of this every day. Not having much is one thing, but having less than others is a bit like feeling that you're bottom of the class – it can make you unhappy. That was why poor people in the country of More (and in all countries for that matter) loved the beach: on the beach people are nearly all equal. Conversely, the rich liked to show that they had more than others, by buying expensive cars they didn't really need, for example.

But Hector wasn't too worried by comparisons. To begin with, he was fortunate enough to belong to a group of people who had more or less everything they wanted. When he was younger, at secondary school, he compared himself with boys who had more success with girls or were better at games, and sometimes it upset him, but since then he'd caught up a bit where girls were concerned, and being good at games isn't all that important when you're a psychiatrist. In general he didn't compare himself very much with others. He knew people who were richer and more famous than he was, but he didn't have the impression that they were any happier. (The proof of this was that some of them had even been to see him to complain about their lives and a few had even tried to kill themselves!) So, he didn't really worry about it that much. Whereas Édouard, for example, often compared himself to people who were richer, but this was normal among businessmen – they're always trying to get ahead.

'Well,' said the professor, 'I think you must be fairly happy, huh? Because a colleague of mine has established that by adding together these three differences – between what we have and what we'd like to have, what we have now and the best of what we've had in the past, and what we have and what other people have – you get an average difference which is closely related to happiness. The smaller the difference the happier we are.'

'But how do you measure happiness?'

'Ah, ah! Good question,' said the professor.

And he began pacing excitedly up and down his study again, his tuft of hair quivering, and Hector remembered that Agnès had told him that measuring happiness was the professor's area of expertise.

And so Hector was very pleased: if he learnt how to measure happiness, he could really say that his trip had been useful!

HECTOR LEARNS HOW TO
MEASURE HAPPINESS

'IMAGINE that I'm a Martian,' said the professor, 'and that I want to understand human beings. How are you going to make me understand that you're feeling happy?'

It was a strange question, worthy of a Martian, Hector thought. Perhaps the professor had shrunk slightly in the space-time machine – except for his nose and his tuft of hair. But Hector also knew that great scholars often had a peculiar way of looking at things, which allowed them to make discoveries. And so he tried to answer as if he were explaining to a Martian what it felt like to be happy.

'Well, I could tell you that I feel good, happy, cheerful, optimistic, positive, in great shape. Obviously if you're a Martian, I'll need to make you understand all those words, to explain to you what emotions are. And emotions are like colours, they're difficult to explain.'

'Absolutely!'

'It might be easier to explain that I'm happy with my life, that things couldn't be going better. That I'm content with my work, my health, my friends, my . . . love life.'

'Not bad! Not bad! What else?'

Hector couldn't think of anything else.

'Have you ever seen a foal in a field in springtime?' the professor asked, abruptly.

Hector had, of course, and the image made him think of Ying Li singing in the bathroom and standing before him smiling and full of life.

'Yes,' Hector said, 'I saw one only recently.'

'And? How did you know that it was happy, huh? You're the Martian now in relation to the young foal.'

This was another peculiar comment, but Hector was beginning to get used to the professor's way of looking at things.

'Yes, I see. I understand that he's happy because he whinnies and capers, and runs about . . . I might smile, sing, laugh, jump for joy, do cartwheels in front of my Martian, and explain that we humans do these things when we're happy. Or at least that while we're doing them we're in a good mood.'

'That's right,' said the professor, 'you've discovered the three main methods of measuring happiness.'

And he explained to Hector that the first method of measuring happiness was to ask people how many times they had felt in a good mood, cheerful, happy during the day or week. The second was to ask them if they were happy in the different areas of their lives. The third was to film people's facial expressions and then measure them in complicated ways. (You could even record a dozen different types of smile, including the smile you have when you're genuinely happy and the smile you give just to show that you're not annoyed when actually you are.)

'We know we're measuring the same thing because if we test a group of people using all three methods and then classify them according to their score, they score more or less the same in all three!'

And the professor looked very pleased when he said this. He looked as if he was about to do cartwheels. Hector remembered Agnès telling him that he'd spent part of his life proving that these three methods of measuring happiness were more or less complementary.

Seeing the professor looking so pleased reminded Hector of lesson no. 10, *Happiness is doing a job you love*, and lesson no. 13, *Happiness is feeling useful to others*. He asked the professor, 'And what do you do with the results?'

'We use them to apply for more grants. I'll be able to begin a new study soon!'

And he began to tell Hector a rather complicated story: he wanted to find out if happiness depended on things going well in people's lives or if it depended above all on their characters – if people were born to be happy, as it were. This was why he had for years been studying a group of young girls (now grown-up women) by asking them every year to fill in lots of questionnaires about how happy they were and what had happened to them during the year, but also by studying their photographs from when they were twenty years old.

'And do you know what?' said the professor. 'There's a relationship between the sincerity and intensity of a smile at twenty years old and happiness at forty!'

Hector would have liked to see the photographs of the young women, but the professor had already begun explaining another study. They'd followed the progress of twins from childhood and tried to discover whether they were both equally happy, even when afterwards they'd led very different lives. It required doing lots of calculations, of the kind Alan liked.

The professor began to explain the calculations on a blackboard and Hector told him not to trouble himself, but the professor insisted. 'Yes, yes, you'll see, you'll understand, huh?' Hector told himself that he was a bit like those skiers who take you up the steep slopes and tell you you'll have great fun, as described at the beginning.

Hector was getting a little tired, and so he asked, 'Has anyone done any calculations on the lessons on my list?'

The professor turned around, irritated. 'Yes, yes, that's what I was about to show you.'

He looked at Hector's list and told him that, thanks to a lot of studies and calculations, they'd shown that if you compared yourself to others and didn't find yourself wanting, if you had no money or health problems, if you had friends, a close-knit family, a job you liked, if you were religious and practised your religion, if you felt useful, if you went for a little stroll from time to time, and all of this in a country that was run by not very bad people, where you were taken care of when things went wrong, your chances of being happy were greatly increased.

Hector was pleased: according to what the professor said, he had every chance of being happy. Apart from the fact that he didn't exactly have a close family, and wasn't very religious – still less was somebody who practised his religion. On the other hand, he knew a lot of people who were married and lived in a perpetual hell of arguments or eternal boredom, and among his patients were very religious people who practised their religion and were very unhappy because they always thought they were bad even when they were being very good. He told this to the professor.

'Well I can't help that!' said the professor. 'These are our findings. Single men are much less happy than married men and for that matter they have more health problems. And according to all our estimates religious people who practise their religion are happier than everybody else. Of course all this is true on average and may not be true in individual cases. But look at all the studies that have been done!'

And he showed Hector a large cupboard containing stacks of papers. These were hundreds of articles written by people like the professor, or Agnès.

Hector felt rather proud at having discovered with the sole aid of his little notebook what people like the professor or Agnès had discovered after carrying out lots of complicated studies. But that's science: it isn't enough just to think a thing, you must try to verify whether it's true. Otherwise people could think and say what they liked, and if those people were fashionable, then everybody would believe them. (Hector recalled that there'd been quite a few fashionable people like that in psychiatry, who liked thinking, and especially talking, but who hated verifying. And as a result they'd said quite a lot of silly things.)

'Well,' said the professor, 'now I'm going to show you something really interesting.'

He took Hector down to the basement. They walked into a large tiled room. In the middle was a huge, rather complicated-looking contraption and an armchair hooked up to some enormous machines that were humming above it, and Hector told himself that this was it, this was a space-time machine and the professor was going to take him on a tour of Mars.

HECTOR DOESN'T GO
TO MARS

STANDING next to the machine was a lady in a white coat. She wore glasses and looked a bit like a schoolmistress, but when you got closer you could see that she was quite pretty.

'My dear Rosalyn!' the professor said.

He seemed all excited, well, even more excited than before.

'My dear John . . .' the lady replied, smiling.

'I've brought you an ideal subject for your experiment: a psychiatrist!' the professor said, introducing Hector.

'Experiment?' asked Hector.

'Yes, but don't worry, it's completely harmless. Come along, Rosalyn hasn't got all day, there's a very long queue!'

And Hector found himself sitting in the armchair surrounded by the machines humming above his head. He saw Rosalyn and the professor, who were standing behind a window in front of a control panel that was as complicated as the one in a big plane.

'Now,' said the professor, 'I'm going to ask you to think of three situations in any order: you're going to imagine yourself in a situation that makes you very happy, in a situation that makes you very sad, and lastly in one where you've felt very scared. It's easier to choose from memories. I'll tell you when you can begin imagining the first situation. But don't, whatever you do, tell me which one it is!'

Hector preferred to begin with the worst. And so he imagined himself sitting in the storeroom that smelt of dead rat, thinking about the people he loved whom he was never going to see again and who would also be very sad. He remembered it so clearly that he felt his eyes prick with tears, even though when he'd been in the real situation he hadn't even cried.

'Good,' said the professor, 'now imagine the second situation.'

This time, Hector imagined that he was watching Clara sleeping. As she worked so hard, she would often sleep in on Sundays. And he would wake up before her and he loved watching her sleeping; it made him very happy, and at moments like those he felt that nothing could go wrong between them.

(You might be wondering why he didn't think of Ying Li. Well, because it didn't make him feel exactly happy thinking of Ying Li so far away in China.)

'Good,' said the professor, 'and now the third situation.'

And Hector pictured himself on the old plane that was vibrating and whirring, with the ducks and chickens making a lot of noise before they landed.

'All right, we're done,' said Rosalyn.

Hector climbed out of the armchair, taking care not to bang his head, and the professor said to him, 'First you thought of the situation that made you sad, then the one that made you happy and finally the one when you were scared.'

Hector knew that the professor would be able to tell (he had heard about this type of machine) but he was still surprised.

The professor took Hector over to the complicated-looking

control panel while Rosalyn turned a few knobs. An image appeared on a colour monitor.

'Look,' the professor said, 'look!'

It looked like an intricate stain made up of lots of pretty colours ranging from very dark blue to bright orange. In fact, it was a photograph of Hector's brain, as though somebody had taken a very fine slice and spread it out flat on a piece of glass.

'This is a map of the oxygen consumption in your brain. The blue areas aren't consuming much. The orange areas, in contrast, are very active.'

Rosalyn pressed some more buttons and three smaller images of Hector's brain appeared in a row. It was clear that in each one different parts of the brain were active.

'Sadness, happiness and fear,' said the professor, pointing at each image. 'Fabulous, isn't it?'

'Happiness is in this area, then,' Hector said, pointing to a little orange spot glowing on the screen, 'on the right side of the brain.'

'Because you're a man,' said Rosalyn. 'In women the area is more diffuse, on both sides of the brain. And similarly when they're sad, for that matter.'

She explained to Hector that since they'd begun using this kind of machine, they'd realised that the brains of men and women didn't work in quite the same way, even when they read or did calculations. Everybody had suspected this for a long time, mind you. But, as previously mentioned, science is about verifying things.

'Imagine if we discovered a drug that activated that area,' Hector said; 'we'd be permanently happy.'

'But we already have! Rosalyn, could you show him the images of the Japanese men's brains?'

And now three images of Japanese men's brains appeared (you'd have to know beforehand that they were Japanese otherwise it would be difficult to guess).

'Now, look closely,' said the professor.

This time, all the brains were bright orange. Above all, in the happiness area. The Japanese men must have been really happy when these were taken.

'But what is this drug?' Hector asked.

He wanted to try some immediately and even take some home for Clara.

'It's saké,' said Rosalyn. 'These were taken a few minutes after they'd drunk a large glass of saké.'

Well, thought Hector, that explained why everybody felt so good when they drank saké or beer or champagne or the wines Édouard liked.

'But look at the next ones,' Rosalyn added. 'These images were taken three hours later.'

Here, the Japanese men's brains looked bluer than at the outset. They even looked like images of sadness. The Japanese men can't have been in very good shape when these were taken. When you saw these images you almost wanted to give them more saké to reactivate their brains (some people have worked all this out on their own without the need for this type of experiment).

Rosalyn also showed Hector images of the brains of men who'd been shown pictures of very beautiful women, and women who were only pretty. And, well, when they saw the very beautiful women, the areas that were activated in these men's brains were the same ones that go very bright after taking the harmful drug produced by Eduardo! This confirmed Hector's idea that you should beware of beauty, but, alas, it was so difficult!

Rosalyn explained that with this type of machine you could find out lots of things about the way healthy people's brains worked, but also about the way they worked when people were sick, and which areas drugs affected. She even showed Hector the effect psychotherapy had on somebody who was very scared of going out of his house. After therapy – which consisted of gradually getting him used to going out again – the images of his brain had gone back to normal!

Hector said that he found this very interesting. He was glad he knew which bit of his brain was being activated when he was happy.

'In fact, your images are like seeing the brain smile.'

Rosalyn and the professor looked at one another.

'The brain smiling!' said the professor. 'What a nice idea!'

And he explained to Hector that these images were very useful for knowing how the brain worked, but that they didn't explain happiness any more than your smile explains why you are happy.

Hector noticed that Rosalyn was smiling as she listened to him. Earlier, when they'd been looking at the images on the screen, out of the corner of his eye he'd seen the professor and Rosalyn kiss.

Which proves, in case you still had any doubts, that the professor definitely wasn't a Martian.

HECTOR WITNESSES AN
EXPERIMENT

THE professor took Hector to lunch outside at one of the university cafés, because in this town the weather was always good except for two weeks in winter when you had to put on a sweater in the evening.

They were sitting facing a huge lawn and Hector was enjoying watching the squirrels, which weren't afraid of people and came up to beg for food. At the other tables were students, students and professors, professors and professors, all mixed together, because it was the kind of university where students and professors talk to each other.

'Well,' the professor said, tucking into his chicken, 'do you feel that you know more about happiness?'

Hector said that he did, but, right at that moment, he felt something tugging at his trouser leg: it was a squirrel wanting some of his lunch. And this made him think. Did the squirrel realise how lucky he was to be there? Or on the contrary did he spend his life wondering whether he might not be better off somewhere else, or feeling that he didn't have the life he deserved? In the end, it depended on the comparisons the squirrel was able to make: he must have seen the large portion of fried squid on the plate in front of Hector. The squirrel could either think that the large portion was a stroke of luck because it increased his chances of getting some squid, or he could consider it a terrible injustice that Hector should have such a large portion all to himself; or he might even feel that it proved that he, the squirrel, was a miserable wretch (especially if his squirrel-wife reminded him of it every evening when he went home). The squirrel's happiness depended on how he looked at things.

So Hector said to the professor, 'Among my patients are people with no money or health problems, who have close-knit families, interesting and useful jobs, but who are quite unhappy: they are fearful about the future, dissatisfied with themselves, they see only the bad side of their situation. There was one determinant of happiness missing from your list just now: people's way of looking at things. In short, people whose glass is always half full are clearly happier than those whose glass is always half empty.'

'Aha!' said the professor. 'That's a typical psychiatrist's observation. But you're right, it's an important point.'

And he explained to Hector that there was a big debate among professors of Happiness Studies. There were those who thought that you were happy above all because your life was full of positive things or events, like in Hector's list. Other professors disagreed: they thought that happiness depended above all on your way of looking at things, on that idea of the glass being half full or half empty.

'Colleagues of mine who defend the second idea tend to think that happiness levels are a bit like blood pressure or weight: they may vary from time to time according to circumstances, but generally they return to the same basic level, which is different in each individual. They study people who have experienced great success or great misfortune and observe that after a few months their moods return more or less to what they were before.'

'And what do you think?' Hector asked.

'A little of both. We depend on circumstance, but some people have more of a gift for happiness than others.'

And Hector thought of Djamila, who was so ill that it was a great misfortune, but who was still happy when she thought that her younger brothers weren't going to die in the war.

Hector took out his little notebook and wrote down a lesson, which he thought was very important:

Lesson no. 20: Happiness is a certain way of seeing things.

The professor was vigorously chewing his chicken. Hector had only ever seen him in a good mood. And this made him ask another question.

'And why do some people have more of a gift for happiness than others?'

The professor went back to the studies of the twins and the young women, but luckily there was no blackboard and so he couldn't begin explaining the calculations again. Basically, having a gift for happiness was a bit like being good at maths or games: it depended partly on the development of the brain after you were born, and even before, but also on how your parents or other adults had brought you up when you were small. And of course on your own efforts and subsequent encounters.

'Nature or nurture,' said the professor. 'Whichever way, the parents are to blame!'

This made him laugh loudly, and the people sitting near them turned around, but when they saw that it was the professor, it made them smile – they all knew him.

Just then, they saw Rosalyn arrive, only she was no longer wearing a white coat, but a pretty blue flowery summer dress; she was talking to an attractive man who kept looking at her, and they went and sat down together at a table.

The professor stopped talking. Hector could see that his good humour had vanished. He turned pale as he watched Rosalyn and the man begin eating their lunch, chatting and smiling.

'That bastard Rupert,' muttered the professor through gritted teeth.

He looked very unhappy and very angry and Hector knew that at moments like this it was good to talk. And so he asked the professor why Rupert was a bastard.

'Not only does he steal my research grants, but he's always hovering around Rosalyn!' replied the professor.

And he explained that, like him, Rupert was a professor, specialising in the difference between men and women's brains. He used Rosalyn's machine quite a lot for his experiments, and so he saw her fairly often.

'And because the difference between men and women is fashionable, the media are interested in what he does and Rupert appears on women's TV programmes. The dean likes that, it's good for the university, and so he gets the biggest research grants in the department.'

And Hector could see the professor suffering as he watched Rosalyn and Rupert chatting and laughing.

Hector took a mental note of a lesson he would write down later:

Lesson no. 21: Rivalry poisons happiness.

If you thought about it, people had always suffered because of rivalries, and had even gone to war: they wanted something the other had or to take the boss's place.

Fortunately, right at that moment Agnès arrived, and this served as a distraction. She was also wearing a nice dress, and when he saw her looking so pretty and smiling, Hector wondered whether he would be happier now if they'd been married when they were young. But perhaps they'd have argued about the children or grown bored of seeing one another all the time and would be divorced by now like everybody else.

'So,' said Agnès, sitting down beside them, 'is Hector's brain normal?'

Hector replied, 'Normal for a psychiatrist,' and this made Agnès laugh, though not the professor, who was trying not to look at Rupert and Rosalyn, but was clearly still suffering. Since Agnès was clever, she immediately understood what was going on. And so she moved opposite the professor, so that at least he couldn't see Rupert and Rosalyn. And she started talking to him about a recent article she'd read on the difference between feeling joy, being in a good mood and happiness, and the professor quickly became excited again and his good mood came back.

Hector gave the squirrel a piece of squid, and it went off to nibble it at a safe distance. Hector didn't know how to read a squirrel's smile, but he had the feeling that the squirrel was quite happy.

And then he looked at Agnès, who had managed to help the professor recover his good mood, and thought again of Djamila, who was happy for her younger brothers, and Ying Li, who sent money to her family, and Marie-Louise's cousin, who had given him that nice surprise. And he made a note:

Lesson no. 22: Women care more than men about making others happy.

He didn't know whether Rupert had already discovered this difference between men and women, but Hector didn't need Rosalyn's machine to know that it was true.

And so might the next lesson be:

Lesson no. 23: Happiness means making sure that those around you are happy?

HECTOR RETRACES HIS
STEPS

'YOU'VE done a fine job,' said the old monk.

He was sitting behind his desk reading Hector's list. He had put on a little pair of glasses, and looked even smaller and older than Hector remembered, but he still looked just as contented.

Hector had copied out his list again after adding on the final lessons, because you couldn't show a rough draft covered in crossings out and nonsensical squiggles to a venerable, kind old monk.

Out of the window, you could still see the magnificent Chinese mountains, occasionally darkened by the shadows of the clouds then dazzling in the sunlight, and Hector thought that seeing the mountains like that every day must help you in some measure to be wise.

The old monk read the list very attentively, and this had a strange effect on Hector. Because the old monk had obviously experienced many more things than he had. And during all his years as a monk he'd also had a lot of time to reflect. And yet he was reading Hector's little lessons on happiness so attentively. Hector wondered whether he himself was capable of reading so attentively the letters his patients sent him, or even those written to him by people he loved.

That could be another lesson: *Be very attentive towards others.*

The old monk stopped reading. He asked Hector to show him his notebook, because he also wanted to see the rough draft. Hector hesitated, and began to say, 'Do you really think . . .' but the old monk laughed, still holding out his hand, and Hector passed him the notebook.

The old monk examined the rough draft. From time to time he smiled, not in a mocking way, as previously mentioned, but because he was genuinely happy. Hector thought to himself that the old monk must have a good way of looking at things, one of the ways that make you happy.

Finally, he stopped reading and asked Hector what it was he had crossed out so thoroughly. Hector felt embarrassed, he didn't really want to tell a monk, but the old monk insisted and so Hector said, *'Lesson no. 18: Happiness could be the freedom to love more than one woman at the same time.'*

The old monk roared with laughter.

'That's what I thought when I was a young man!'

He closed the notebook, looked at the list again and then he said, 'You really have done a fine job. All your lessons are very good. I have nothing to add.'

Hector was pleased but at the same time a little disappointed. He'd been hoping the old monk would provide him with a few more lessons, or at least a good theory about happiness.

The old monk looked at him again, smiling, and added, 'It's a beautiful day, let's go for a walk.'

Outside, the scenery was magnificent. They could see mountains, sea, sky.

Hector felt a little daunted being on his own with the venerable old monk, and he didn't really know what to say. But at the same time, he sensed that the old monk wasn't expecting him to say anything particularly intelligent or wise, that he simply wanted to share this immense beauty with him.

The old monk said, 'True wisdom would be the ability to live without this scenery, to be the same person even at the bottom of a well. But that, it has to be said, is not so easy.'

And Hector understood that he'd experienced this, at the bottom of a well.

For a moment, they watched the clouds, the sun and the wind play over the mountains. Hector wondered whether this wasn't another lesson: *Take time to observe the beauty of the world.*

Just then, a young monk came up the little path towards them. He said something in Chinese to the old monk, and went back down to the monastery gardens, where you could see other monks gardening (a special type of gardening that looks easy, but is difficult to explain).

'Well,' said the old monk, 'there's a visitor waiting for me. But I'm glad that we've been able to spend a little time together.'

Ever since he'd arrived, Hector had been longing to ask a question, and now he took the plunge.

'The first time we met, you said to me: it's a mistake to think that happiness is the goal. I'm not sure I understand.'

'I was referring to the goals which you in your civilisation are so good at setting yourselves, and which incidentally allow you to achieve many interesting things. But happiness is a different thing altogether. If you try to achieve it, you have every chance of failing. And besides, how would you ever know that you'd achieved it? Of course one can't blame people, especially unhappy people, for wanting to be happier and setting themselves goals in order to try to escape from their unhappiness.'

'Do you mean that the same lessons don't apply to everybody?'

The old monk looked at Hector and said, 'Do you tell all your patients the same thing?'

Hector thought for a moment and said that he didn't, that it depended on their character, on whether they were young or old, on whether they'd experienced true unhappiness or not.

'There you are, you see,' the old monk said. 'It's the same thing.'

Then Hector thought about it a little more and said that although he didn't tell all his patients the same thing, even so there were certain basic principles that he often returned to, especially with people who were sad or scared: he helped them distinguish between what they thought, about themselves and others, and reality. Because they tended to believe that what they thought was reality and that was often not the case.

'There you go, it's still the same thing. Let's go back now.'

He walked back towards the monastery, and Hector followed, wondering what he'd meant.

When they reached the entrance to the monastery, the old monk told him to wait there for a moment, as he had something to give him. A Chinese man was waiting and Hector realised that this was the visitor the young monk had come to tell the old monk about earlier. But the man wasn't dressed like a monk, more like someone from the city, in a suit and tie.

On this trip, Hector had formed the habit of talking to people he didn't know. And so he introduced himself to the

Chinese man, who spoke better English than Hector. They realised that they were both doctors, and that the Chinese man was a specialist, like the ones mentioned earlier but not named so as not to worry you.

The old monk returned. He was holding two beautiful blue and white Chinese bowls with a pretty design on them. He said to Hector, 'They are wedding bowls. You may give them away . . . or keep them.'

And he gave his little laugh again and then said goodbye to Hector.

On the doorstep, Hector turned around and saw the old monk and the Chinese doctor looking at him, and the old monk gave him a last smile and raised his hand to wave at him, and it reminded him of Djamila.

Outside, it was still a beautiful day, but Hector felt a little sad.

He stopped to put the Chinese bowls in his bag. He didn't want to risk them breaking. Between the two bowls was a tiny scrap of paper. On it was written: 20–13–10.

Hector took out his little notebook and read:

Lesson no. 20: Happiness is a certain way of seeing things.

Lesson no. 13: Happiness is feeling useful to others.

Lesson no. 10: Happiness is doing a job you love.

Hector told himself that these were quite good lessons. For him in any case.

HECTOR INVENTS THE GAME OF
THE FIVE FAMILIES

'CALIFORNIAN, French or Chilean?'
'Which do you prefer?'

Hector and Édouard were in that fine restaurant where you could see the city lights shining and the boats in the bay, and they were talking as though they'd seen each other only yesterday, which is how it is between real friends.

While they were waiting for the Chinese wine waiter, Édouard asked Hector whether he had learnt anything that might be useful to him, Édouard. Hector had noticed that Édouard looked pleased to see him again, but not especially happy, just as before. He thought that he might be able to help him with some good advice.

'Well, to start with, there are various types of happiness. Let's call them families of happiness.'

'That doesn't surprise me,' said Édouard, 'but what are they?'

'Let's say there are five families. First, two families of exciting happiness and two families of calm happiness. Exciting happiness is joy, celebration, travelling, being in bed with a woman you desire.'

'Ah, I know that kind of happiness! And does it include this?' he asked, pointing at the bottle which the Chinese wine waiter had just brought.

Hector said that it did, of course, and he told him about the brains of the Japanese men who'd drunk saké, and that it was like seeing the brain smile. Édouard didn't say anything, but Hector could see that it had made him think.

'The second family of exciting happiness is doing a job you like, wanting to attain a goal. This could be in your work, but also in sport or gardening or even thinking about a complicated calculation if that's what you like.'

He explained to Édouard how Alan liked running and doing calculations, and how Jean-Michel loved doing his job, which was caring for sick children and mothers, and how excited the professor became when he tried to understand happiness.

'Hmm,' said Édouard, 'I feel some of that happiness when I'm working on an interesting acquisition and I manage to convince the client. But it doesn't excite me much any more . . .'

'And then there are the two families of calm happiness. The first is simply feeling contented and wanting that to last. That's when you make comparisons and discover that you're happy as you are by comparison with others or with your own past. Or when you don't compare yourself with anything at all!'

He told him about Agnès, who compared herself now to how she'd been before and thought that she'd never been as happy, even though things weren't perfect. He told him about the children in Marie-Louise's country who weren't old enough yet to make comparisons.

'That doesn't work for me,' replied Édouard, 'I'm always comparing myself to others.'

'To people who've earned six million dollars?'

'Yes, and when I've earned six million, to people who've earned twenty million.'

'It's a particular way of seeing things,' said Hector. 'You don't compare yourself to the women on the oilcloth?'

'Alas, no! I compare myself to people like me.'

He tasted the wine and said, 'Not bad, but I prefer the '76 we had last time. And the second family of calm happiness?'

'Just that. It's a certain way of seeing things. Cultivating your serenity and keeping hold of it whatever happens, even in the face of your own death.'

Édouard turned pale.

'You think I'm going to die soon?'

'No, of course not; I was speaking generally.'

And he told him about Djamila on the plane and about the old monk on the mountain.

Édouard listened very attentively to Hector. And then he said that he understood why he didn't feel very happy.

'Partying doesn't interest me like it did before, my job occasionally excites me, but, as I've already told you, I don't really like it. I constantly compare myself to people who have more than I do. And on top of that I don't feel in the slightest bit serene. I get irritated as soon as things don't go the way I want.'

'There's a fifth family of happiness.'

'Ah, perhaps that's my last chance . . .'

'It is happiness that comes from others: friendship, mutual love, caring about other people's happiness or unhappiness, feeling useful to others.'

'That can also be a great source of unhappiness!' said

Édouard. 'People let you down, your friends betray you. As for love, you sometimes get badly hurt.'

This reminded Hector that Édouard must have been in love, but that it can't have gone well.

'That's true, but being with other people and their imperfections can also bring serenity, the happiness of the fourth family. And besides, you can feel useful to others without necessarily expecting gratitude and still be happy.'

Édouard looked at Hector.

'You sound like a monk.'

This made Hector laugh. And suddenly he wondered whether he wasn't starting to laugh like the old monk. So he added, 'I'm going to prove to you that it isn't true, that I don't yet sound entirely like a monk.'

And he asked Édouard for news of Ying Li.

You were expecting this, of course. Hector couldn't come back to China just to talk to the old monk and Édouard, and not bother about Ying Li any more!

Édouard told him that Ying Li was still working at the bar with the soft lighting, and that he saw her from time to time. Once, she had asked him about Hector.

'I'm not sure I should have told you that,' said Édouard.

Of course he should, though at the same time Hector felt a pang when he imagined Ying Li asking about him.

It hasn't been mentioned for a while, but Hector had never really stopped thinking about Ying Li – in fact he thought about her several times a day and when he woke up in the night. To begin with, he'd thought of saving Ying Li from her job and taking her to his country, because those are the two things you want to do most when you love somebody: to save them (sometimes from themselves) and to be near them always. After that, Hector had had time to reflect when he was in the storeroom that smelt of dead rat, and he'd realised how much he loved Clara. And then later, he'd sort of become his own psychiatrist and had examined his love for Ying Li. He knew his love for her was more a desire to save her, to be her superhero, and it was partly a desire to do what people who are in love do, and partly a desire to feel young again with her, because Ying Li was very young, and she looked even younger.

Hector had seen quite a few love affairs like that in his life and in his work, and he knew that they didn't always turn out very well. In his country, Ying Li would be incapable of doing anything without him, he would constantly be saving her, and it wasn't necessarily the best thing for love, even though it was often very exciting at the beginning.

Hector had thought about all of this, but more than anything, as previously mentioned, he had realised that it was Clara he loved, and that he loved her in many different ways. (Because there are even more ways of loving than there are ways of being happy, but it would take another book to explain them all.)

And so Hector said to Édouard, 'I'm going to introduce you to the fifth family of happiness. Do you have your mobile with you?'

Of course he did. Édouard always had his mobile with him and he gave it to Hector.

And so Hector phoned Eduardo.

HECTOR'S JOURNEY IS A
GREAT SUCCESS

Hector had returned to his country and had gone back to being a psychiatrist. But his trip had changed his way of working quite a lot.

He still gave pills to people who needed them, and he still tried to help people get better using psychotherapy. But he had incorporated a new method into his psychotherapy.

For example, when a well-dressed lady – a lady who always looked very stern like a wicked schoolmistress – complained that nobody liked her, Hector began telling her about the little children begging, who smiled all the time, and he asked the woman why she thought they smiled.

Or when a man came to see him who was always worried about his health although he had nothing seriously wrong with him, Hector told him the story of Djamila on the plane, who knew that she was going to die soon, and he asked the man why he thought she smiled and why she sometimes even felt happy.

He also told them about the old monk, the party at Marie-Louise's house, Alan who liked doing calculations, the squirrel waiting for his fried squid and about many other things that had happened to him during his trip, and even things you haven't been told about. But Hector never told them the endings of the stories, he always asked people to find out for themselves and this made them think and some of them came back the next time saying that they'd understood something very important.

To Adeline, who complained a lot about men, he told the story of how Agnès realised that she was happy. This didn't work so well, because it irritated Adeline that Hector should waste time talking about some other woman rather than her. After which, she asked him whether Alan was a celebrity over there because of his puzzles, and Hector realised that there was still a lot of work to do.

He saw Roger and Madame Irina again, too.

Roger was very happy because those whose job it was to help people like him had signed him up to go on a pilgrimage. Perhaps Roger would need less medication during that period.

Madame Irina told him that she had only come to say goodbye, because she was able to see into the future again. She looked at Hector.

'Oh, oh, Doctor, I can see that you were a bit naughty when you were in China.'

Hector replied that this wasn't true at all, that on the contrary he had attained wisdom in China, but this made Madame Irina laugh.

Of course he hadn't talked to her about Ying Li; in fact he never talked to anybody about Ying Li, except occasionally to Édouard on the telephone. Because Ying Li wasn't working at the bar with soft lighting any more, she was working for Édouard, helping him with his projects at the bank. Édouard said that she was doing very well, because the advantage of being young is that you learn very fast, even when you've fallen behind as a child, as in Ying Li's case.

You're wondering how this could be, because you remember

the tall Chinese man and the lady in the car who scowled at Ying Li that evening when she went out with Hector. Ying Li was worth a lot to those people, and what's more she wasn't for sale, you could only hire her if you were a client. Here's what happened.

In the restaurant, Hector had called Eduardo from Édouard's mobile phone. There's something else you should know: when Hector was in the country of More, Eduardo had called him to discuss his wife. (At the time Hector had wondered how Eduardo had known that he was staying with Alan and Agnès, but later Clara told him that while he was there, a friend with a Spanish accent had called her office to ask where Hector was. Since Hector had never spoken of Clara to Eduardo either, this didn't make things any clearer, but, as previously mentioned, sometimes it's better not to know the whole story.)

On the telephone, Eduardo had told Hector that his wife was feeling much better since she'd started taking the pills Hector had recommended, and even better still since she'd started seeing the psychiatrist he'd told them about.

'It's wonderful,' Eduardo said. 'I've got my wife back. I feel as if I'm living again with the woman I knew before she was ill!'

And he told Hector that he owed him a great deal and that he'd like to give him a gift. And people like Eduardo know a bit about gifts. But Hector told him that he might prefer a favour, a favour that would also be a gift, but that he needed a little more time to think about it. Eduardo said that was okay, he could do Hector any favour he wanted.

And so when Hector called Eduardo, he asked him the

favour. And Eduardo said, 'No problem.' Incidentally, he also knew the bar with the soft lighting from his business trips to China. Hector imagined the tall Chinese man's expression when they told him that Ying Li didn't belong to him now. It gave him great pleasure, because he remembered how he'd spoken to Ying Li when they'd left the bar and it had made him very angry, and he'd thought about it many times since.

And that's the end of the story.

Ying Li continued to work for Édouard, and she made a lot of progress and one day she met a young man her own age from Hector's country, who was doing his military service in China (the sort of military service children of well-dressed people do) and they got married. Later, they had a baby and they made Édouard godfather. Ying Li wanted to call the baby Édouard, but Édouard said that he preferred Eduardo because that way people wouldn't get them mixed up, and so that's what the baby was called.

Édouard felt a little bit happier, perhaps because he'd discovered the fifth family of happiness, perhaps also because he occasionally went to see the old monk at the monastery. (Hector had given him the address.) The old monk was growing more and more frail and more and more tired, but he still laughed occasionally when he spoke to Édouard.

Finally, Édouard left his job, just before he'd earned his six million dollars. He carried on working in roughly the same profession as before, but free of charge. He worked to help good people in countries like Marie-Louise's find money so that their children could go to school or receive medical treatment. And he worked to find ways of getting loans for grown-ups so that they could get jobs and earn the money to send their children to school or to pay for their medical treatment. Édouard really loved his new job. He had replaced lesson no. 4: *Many people think that happiness comes from having more power or more money* with lesson no. 13: *Happiness is feeling useful to others.* You might say that there wasn't much merit in this because Édouard was already rich from earning his six million dollars, but you must understand that in Édouard's eyes he wasn't rich, because he knew quite a lot of people who'd earned at least twenty million and all they could think about was earning even more.

One day, Hector received a letter from Djamila's sister. In the letter was a beautiful photograph of Djamila from before she was ill, smiling the way people smile when they're happy. The sister explained that Djamila had told them about Hector. She had never forgotten what Hector had done for her and had wanted them to send the photograph to him when she was no longer there.

Jean-Michel continued to treat babies and their mothers, and Alan to do calculations and go running every morning, Agnès continued to study other people's children and bring up her own very well, and the squirrel continued going to the café every lunchtime. But you must have understood that these people were already relatively happy before this story began, except perhaps for the important professor, who still suffered occasionally because of Rupert and Rosalyn. Hector also thought of Marie-Louise's cousin from time to time, and he even saw her again one day when she was visiting his country. This time they were very well behaved and only had lunch. Because there are times when getting up to mischief isn't mischievous and other times when it is and you shouldn't do it.

Hector continued seeing people who were very sad or very scared or who had experienced real misfortune or who suffered from none of these things but who were unhappy anyway. But since his trip, he loved his job even more, and he loved Clara more, too. And as a result, Clara became less interested in her meetings and stopped bringing work home at the weekends and began looking at babies when she saw them with their mothers in the street. And Hector noticed this and thought that one day he and Clara might get married, live happily and have many children.

ACKNOWLEDGEMENTS

I would like to thank my friends and their families for the hospitality they showed me during my visits to their countries prior to Hector's journey: Hans and Elisabeth, Peter and Margaret, Bob and his team at UCLA, Siew and Khai, Marie-Joséphine and Cyril. Many thanks also to Étienne for having introduced me to the Middle Kingdom, and to Nicolas for making himself available and being such an excellent guide. I am similarly grateful to the Aviation Medical Assistance Act, which now protects doctors who provide medical assistance during commercial flights. I would also like to extend my gratitude to everybody at Éditions Odile Jacob, and in particular to the readers of Hector's earliest adventures: Jean-Luc Fidel, Catherine Meyer, Cécile Andrier, Jean-Jérôme Renucci. My special thanks to my publishers Odile Jacob and Bernard Gottlieb for having welcomed and supported this book, so different from my former ones.

Francois Lelord on
Hector and the Search for Happiness

Q. Do people really need a guide to happiness?

The first books I ever wrote were non-fiction psychology books which were sort of guides to daily life. But when I was writing *Hector* I didn't feel the need to produce a practical guide to love and happiness. These are emotional subjects that can't just be carved up into chapters, rules and lessons. So I chose to write these fables or novels in the hope that readers might learn something about themselves and love or happiness in a more personal kind of way. I truly believe that Hector's adventures make more of an impact on readers than a straightforward practical guide which offers advice at the end of each chapter.

Q. So do we know how to recognise happiness?

In the first *Hector* novel which deals with happiness, the hero states that people have a tendency to ruin moments of happiness. We compare our present situation to our past experiences, or to the situation or experiences of others. To really savour a moment of happiness, one has to try and forget about the past and other people. If one is constantly making comparisons, it's hard to ever feel happy.

Q. Nowadays, people always want more: they want to be younger, more beautiful, richer. Why is this?

We always want more because happiness has become a value. For a long time, life was ruled by duty: one had to fulfil one's duty as a mother, wife, husband, soldier . . . Happiness was something that came on top, but only after you had done your duty. A sense of guilt at being a bad father or mother was the worst feeling you could have. But since the end of the Second World War, personal fulfilment has turned into a value. In the 1970s, the search for happiness became the number one priority for everyone. But if one is overly concerned with one's happiness, one risks increasing the chances of being unhappy. It's about finding a balance between self-abnegation and total egotism.

Q. Are people happier in rich societies?

Studies show that below a certain level of poverty, it's very hard to be happy. However, once basic needs have been met and if one also lives in a community of people with a roughly similar standard of living, being 'richer' doesn't significantly increase happiness. Poor people who live in poor countries are much happier than poor people living in wealthier countries. In fact what's most important is to feel acceptance amongst one's social group.

Hector and the Secrets of Love

The second of Hector's Journeys

François Lelord

Following the search for happiness in his first journey, Hector, the celebrated young psychiatrist, is to embark on a new adventure.

What if the secret of love were to lie in a particular combination of molecules? Genial Professor Cormoran, a world expert on love, has disappeared, and he's taken the results of his latest research with him!

Hector, who is forever dealing with the casualties of love in his consulting rooms, is charged with finding the professor . . . He sets off on a journey that will take him as far as China, where he too will experience misfortune in love.

Will he escape the clutches of his pursuers? Will he find Professor Cormoran and his amazing discovery, which could change the course of human history? Will he succumb to the charms of sweet Vayla or will he be reconciled with his dear Clara?

But, above all, will his journey help him understand the mysteries of love a little better?

A tender and enlightening fable on the emotions.

GALLIC BOOKS

ISBN 978-1-906040-33-8

February 2011

Extract from *Hector and the Secrets of Love*
Coming in February 2011
ISBN 978-1-906040-33-8
£7.99

'ALL we have to say to him is: "My dear doctor, you're going to help us to discover the secret of love." I'm sure he'll consider it a very noble mission.'

'Do you think he's up to it?'

'Yes, I think so.'

'He'll need persuading – you have the necessary funds.'

'More importantly, I think we need to make him feel he'll be doing something worthwhile.'

'So, we'll need to tell him everything?'

'Yes. Well, not everything, if you see what I mean.'

'Of course.'

Two men in grey suits were in discussion late at night in a very big office at the top of a tall building. Through the picture windows the bright city lights shone as far as the eye could see, but they didn't take any notice of them.

They were too busy looking at the photographs in the file in front of them – glossy portraits of a youngish-looking man with a dreamy expression.

'Psychiatrist, what a strange occupation!' said the older man. 'I wonder how they can stand it.'

'Yes, I wonder, too.'

The younger man, a tall, strapping fellow with cold eyes, replaced all the photos in the file, which was marked: 'Dr Hector'.

HECTOR AND THE CHINESE PICTURE

O NCE upon a time there was a young psychiatrist called Hector.

Psychiatry is an interesting profession, but it can be very difficult, and even quite tiring. In order to make it less tiring, Hector had made himself a pleasant consulting room and had hung up some of his favourite pictures – in particular one he'd brought back from China. It was a large redwood panel decorated with beautiful Chinese letters – or, for those who like to be precise, ideograms. When Hector felt tired because of all the problems people talked to him about, he would look at the beautiful gilded Chinese letters carved in the wood and he would feel better. The people who sat in the chair opposite him to talk about their problems would sometimes glance at the Chinese panel. It often seemed to Hector that this did them good, that afterwards they appeared calmer.

A few of them asked Hector what the Chinese letters meant, and this made Hector feel awkward because he didn't know. He couldn't read Chinese, still less speak it (even though he'd once met a nice Chinese girl, over in China). When you're a doctor it's never very good to let your patients see that there's something you don't know, because they like to think that you know everything, it reassures them. And so Hector would invent a different saying each time, trying to come up with the one he thought would do most good to the person asking.

For example, to Sophie – a woman who'd been divorced the previous year and was still very angry with the father of her children – Hector explained that the expression in Chinese meant: 'He who spends too long regretting his ruined crop will neglect to plant next year's harvest.'

Sophie had opened her eyes wide and after that she'd almost stopped talking to Hector about what a dreadful man her ex-husband was.

To Roger – a man who had the habit of talking to God in a very loud voice in the street (he believed God talked to him, too, and could even hear his words echoing in his head) – Hector said that the expression meant: 'The wise man is silent when communing with God.'

Roger replied that this was all very well for the god of the Chinese people, but that he, Roger, was talking to the real God, and so it was only normal for him to speak loud and clear. Hector agreed, but added that since God could hear and understand everything, there was no need for Roger to talk to Him out loud, it was enough just to think of Him. Hector was trying to save Roger from getting into trouble when he was out and about, and from being put into hospital for long periods. Roger said that he ended up in hospital so often because it was the will of God, and that suffering was a test of faith.

On one hand, Hector felt that the new treatment he'd prescribed Roger had helped him express himself more clearly and made him a lot more talkative, but on the other, it didn't make Hector's job any less tiring.

In fact, what Hector found most tiring was the question of love. Not in his own life, but in the lives of all those people who came to see him.

Because love, it seemed, was an endless source of suffering.

Some people complained of not having any at all.

'Doctor, I'm bored with my life, I feel so unhappy. I'd really like to be in love, to feel loved. I feel as if love is only for others, not for me.'

This was the sort of thing Anne-Marie would say, for example. When she had asked Hector what the Chinese expression meant, Hector had looked at her very carefully. Anne-Marie could have been pretty if only she'd stopped dressing like her mother and hadn't focused all her energy on her work. Hector replied: 'If you want to catch fish you must go to the river.'

Soon afterwards, Anne-Marie joined a choir. She started wearing make-up and stopped dressing like her mother all the time.

Some people complained of too much love. Too much love was as bad for their health as too much cholesterol.

'It's terrible, I should stop, I know that our relationship is over, but I can't help thinking about him all the time. Do you think I should write to him … or call him? Or should I wait outside his office to try to see him?'

This was Claire, who, as can often happen, had become involved with a man who wasn't free, and to begin with this was fun because, as she told Hector, she wasn't in love, but then she did fall in love, and the man did, too. Even so, they decided to stop seeing one another because the man's wife was becoming suspicious, and he didn't want to leave her. And so Claire suffered a lot, and when she asked Hector what the words on the Chinese panel said, he had to reflect for a moment before coming up with a reply. 'Do not build your home in a neighbour's field.'

Claire had burst into tears and Hector hadn't felt very pleased with himself.

He also saw men who suffered because of love, and these cases were even more serious: men only find the courage to go to a psychiatrist when they're very, very unhappy or when they've exhausted all their friends with their problems and have begun drinking too much.

This was the case with Luc – a boy who was a bit too nice and suffered a lot when women left him, especially as he often chose women who were not very nice, probably because his mother hadn't been very nice to him when he was little. Hector told him that the Chinese panel said: 'If you are scared of the panther, hunt the antelope.' And then he wondered whether there were antelopes in China. Luc replied: 'That's a rather bloodthirsty proverb. The Chinese are quite bloodthirsty, aren't they?'

Hector realised that it wasn't going to be easy.

Some people, very many actually, both men and women, complained of having enjoyed a very loving relationship with someone, but of no longer feeling the same way despite still being very fond of that person, with whom they generally lived.

'I tell myself that maybe it's normal after all these years. On the other hand we get along so well. But we haven't made love for months ... Together, I mean.'

With those cases, Hector had a bit of trouble finding a useful meaning for the Chinese panel, or else he'd come up with clichéd expressions like: 'The wise man sees the beauty of each season,' which meant nothing, even to him.

Some people complained of having love, but for the wrong person.

'Oh dear, I know he'll end up being a disaster just like all the others. But I can't help myself.'

This was Virginie. She went from love affair to love affair with men who were very attractive to women, which was very exciting to begin with, but rather painful in the end. For her, Hector came up with: 'He who hunts must start again each day, while he who cultivates can watch his rice growing.'

Virginie said that it was amazing how much the Chinese managed to say in only four characters, and Hector felt that she was a little bit cleverer than he.

Other people had love, but still found things to worry about.

'We love each other, of course. But is this the right person for me? Marriage isn't to be taken lightly. When you marry it's for life. And anyway, I want to enjoy my freedom a bit longer …'

Hector generally asked these people to tell him about their mothers and fathers and how they got along.

Other people wondered whether they could ever hope to know love, whether it wasn't too good for them.

'I can't imagine anybody finding me attractive. Deep down, I don't think I'm a very interesting person. Even you seem bored, Doctor.'

At this point Hector woke up completely and said, no, not at all, and then kicked himself because the right thing to say would have been: 'What makes you think that?'

So, a lot of people came to explain to Hector that love or lack of love prevented them from sleeping, thinking, laughing, and in some cases even from living. And with those cases, Hector had to be very careful, because he knew that love can make people kill themselves, which is a very foolish thing to do, so don't ever do it and if you have thoughts about doing it go to see someone like Hector immediately, or call a close friend.

Hector had been in love, and he remembered how much suffering love can cause: days and nights spent thinking about somebody who doesn't want to see you any more, wondering whether it would be better to write, to call or to remain in silence, unable to sleep unless you drink everything in the mini-bar of the hotel room in the town you've come to in order to see her except that she doesn't want to see you. Now, of course, this type of memory helped him better understand people who found themselves in the same situation. Another thing which Hector remembered, and which he wasn't very proud of, was the nice girls whom he had made suffer because of love: they had loved him and he had only liked them. Sometimes, he'd lived through both roles, victim and executioner, with the same girl, because love is complicated, and, what's worse, it's unpredictable.

This type of suffering was now a thing of the past for Hector. (Or so he thought at the beginning of this story, but just wait and see.) Because he had a good friend, Clara, whom he loved very much and she loved him, and they were even thinking of having a baby together or of getting married. Hector was happy because in the end love affairs are very tiring, so when you find somebody you love and who loves you, you really hope that it will be your last love affair.

What's strange is that, at the same time, you wonder if it isn't a bit sad to think that it will be your last love affair. You see how complicated love is!

HECTOR LOVES CLARA

ONE evening Hector arrived home, his mind taken up by all the painful stories about love he'd heard during the day: situations in which one person loves more than the other, or both people love each other but they don't get on, or they no longer love each other but can't love anybody else, and other combinations besides, because, just as happiness in love offers a beautiful, relatively unchanging landscape, unhappiness comes in many and varied forms, as a great Russian author once put it slightly better.

Clara wasn't home yet, because she always had meetings that finished late. She worked for a large pharmaceutical company, which produced a lot of the world's leading drugs. The large company often amused itself by eating up smaller companies, and one day it even tried to eat up a company larger than itself, but the larger company fought it off.

Clara's bosses were pleased with her because she was a very conscientious hard-working girl, and they often asked her to stand in for them at meetings or sum up long reports for them, which they hadn't time to read.

Hector was happy to know that Clara's bosses had faith in her, but on the other hand he didn't like her coming home so late, often tired, and not always in a very good mood because, although her bosses depended on her a lot, they never took her along to the really important meetings with the real big shots, they went to those on their own, and made out that they were the ones who had done all the work or come up with all the good ideas.

What a surprise, then, when Clara arrived home with a big smile on her face.

'Good day?' asked Hector, who was happy to see Clara looking so pretty and smiling.

'Oh, not great, too many meetings getting in the way of work. And everybody is in a panic because the patent on our leading drug has expired. So we can kiss our profits goodbye!'

'You look happy, anyway.'

'All the happier for seeing you, my love.'

And she began to laugh. You see, this was Clara's way of jesting about love. Luckily, Hector was used to it and he knew that Clara really loved him.

'Well,' said Clara, 'it's true, but I'm also happy because we've received an invitation.'

'We?'

'Yes, well, you're the one invited, but I'm allowed to go with you.'

Clara took a letter out of her briefcase and gave it to Hector.

'They should really have posted it to you, but they're aware by now that we know each other.'

Hector read the letter. It was written by a man who was very high up in Clara's company, one of the real big shots she didn't meet very often. He said that he thought very highly of Hector (Hector remembered they'd shaken hands twice at conferences on psychiatry) and was relying on him to take part in a confidential meeting, where people from the company would ask his opinion on a very important matter. He hoped that Hector would agree to go, and repeated how much he appreciated him.

Together with the letter was another piece of paper showing the place where the meeting would be held: a very pretty hotel made of wood, on a faraway island, and overlooking a magnificent beach with palm trees. Hector wondered why they had to take them so far. It was perfectly possible to reflect at home in an armchair, but he told himself that this was the company's way of making him feel that he was important to them.

There was a third piece of paper telling Hector that in addition to the invitation he would of course be paid for giving his opinion. When he saw the amount, he thought he'd added on a zero, but on rereading it he realised that he hadn't, that it was right.

'Hasn't there been some mistake?' Hector asked Clara.

'No, that's the correct amount. The others are getting the same – more or less what they asked for.'

'The others?'

She gave Hector the names of his fellow psychiatrists who had also been invited.

Hector knew them. There was a very old psychiatrist with a bow tie who, as he grew older, had specialised in rich unhappy people (though he also occasionally saw poor people and didn't charge them), and a funny little lady who had specialised in people who had difficulty doing what people who are in love do, and who were willing to pay crazy amounts of money in order to be able to do it.

'Right, well, this will be a mini holiday for us,' said Hector.

'Speak for yourself,' said Clara. 'I'll be seeing the same old faces I see at every meeting.'

'At least we'll be going away somewhere together for a change,' said Hector.

'We went to Italy recently!'

'That was only because you had a conference there afterwards. Your job always determines everything.'

'Would you prefer me to be a good little housewife and stay at home?'

'No, I'd prefer you to stop letting yourself be exploited, and come home at a reasonable time.'

'I bring you a piece of good news and you immediately start complaining!'

'You're the one who started it.'

'No I didn't, you did.'

Hector and Clara carried on bickering, and finally went to bed without speaking to each other or kissing each other goodnight. Which just goes to show that love isn't easy, even for psychiatrists.

During the night, Hector woke up. In the dark, he found his luminous pen, which allowed him to write without waking Clara up. He noted: 'Perfect love would be never having to argue.'

He reflected. He wasn't sure.

He didn't feel he could call his expression a 'lesson'. Wanting to give lessons on love seemed a bit ridiculous. He thought of 'reflection', but it was too serious for such a simple phrase. It was only a tiny thought, like a seedling that has just sprouted and nobody knows what it will be yet. There, he'd found it. It was a seedling. He wrote:

Seedling no. 1: Perfect love would be never having arguments.

He reflected for a little bit longer; it was difficult, his eyelids kept closing. He looked at Clara who was sleeping.

Seedling no. 2: Sometimes we argue most with the people we love most.